MURDER AT THE SUMMIT

A BLAKE SISTERS TRAVEL MYSTERY – BOOK 5

CARTER FIELDING

Published by Carter Fielding Press
5237 River Road, #304
Bethesda, MD 20216

Editing, design, and production by Bublish, Inc.

ISBN: 978-1-64704-786-3 eBook
ISBN: 978-1-64704-787-0 paperback

For information about the author and her projects,
please visit:
www.mcarterfielding.com

To Cuyler and Maura, my stalwart champions.
Thanks for never doubting me,
even when I doubt myself.

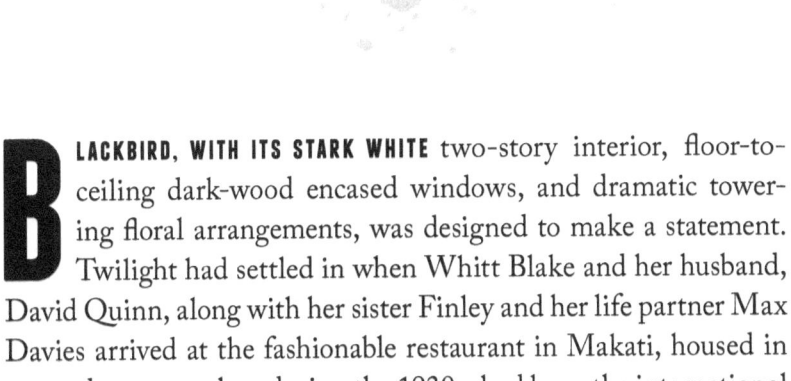

BLACKBIRD, WITH ITS STARK WHITE two-story interior, floor-to-ceiling dark-wood encased windows, and dramatic towering floral arrangements, was designed to make a statement. Twilight had settled in when Whitt Blake and her husband, David Quinn, along with her sister Finley and her life partner Max Davies arrived at the fashionable restaurant in Makati, housed in an art deco space that, during the 1930s, had been the international airport.

Several of the group from the bank where Whitt worked were already seated by the time she and the others walked in. Finley had heard so much about Whitt's bank friends and looked forward to meeting them—Aliyan and Saskia, Rob and Amiko, Francisco and Caroline, and Monica and Jay. Charlie, Whitt's best friend in Manila, rounded out the group, even though she didn't work at the bank.

"You guys heading to Palawan?" Rob had poured himself a glass of wine and leaned back against the chair, his arm resting around his wife Amiko's shoulders. "The diving's some of the best in the world. David knows!"

"I'm excited. David and I are heading out on a charter to El Nido and a few other spots that he says are good," Max explained.

David nodded. "Hoping to get the ladies to join us for at least some snorkeling before they head up to the Summit."

David's comment caught the ladies' attention. And it wasn't because of the snorkeling.

Caroline shifted in her seat and stared at Whitt. "You're going to the Summit? How did you swing that? The waitlist for that place is a mile long!"

Monica agreed. "Daniella, Mark's wife, had her name on the list for almost six months before she finally got in. I'm dying to go." Mark was another of their colleagues at the bank.

"I would be careful using the word 'dying' when these two sisters are together. It can be dangerous!" Max teased as he put his arm around Finley.

"Max says it as a joke, but these two do have a reputation. I don't care where it is in the world—Tangier, Galle, Jaipur. Even Charleston. If Finley and Whitt are together, something deadly is bound to happen," Charlie leaned forward to catch Monica's eye. "I've seen it firsthand!"

"And yet, these two married us anyway!" Whitt took David's arm and kissed his cheek. "Now who's the fool?"

Finley chuckled. It was true. Six months ago, almost to the day, Whitt and David had become husband and wife. And a little over a year before that, Max and Finley had committed to each other forever, their version of "committed permanence without marriage," in deference to Max's aversion to the institution. Somehow both men had managed to overlook the bodies that popped up wherever Finley and Whitt went.

Monica brought the conversation back on topic. "So, what things are you going to have done? Daniella said the specialized treatments were expensive but well worth it. They have an antigravity capsule. Supposed to take years off your face!"

Whitt scoffed, "Daniella isn't even thirty. If she gets any more years taken off, she'll be back in diapers! I'll be staying away from that one." She continued, "No big secret to getting in. I won four days for two at the Summit at the Children's Welfare benefit gala. And this is the weekend. Then Finley got an assignment to write about the best spas in Asia."

Finley interjected, "A difficult mission but someone had to make the sacrifice!"

"David didn't want to go, so Charlie volunteered."

"What I don't do for my friends!" Charlie giggled.

Finley and Whitt could tell that David and Max were as giddy-excited about their diving schedule as two boys heading out on their first fishing trip. Their guide, a short man with a muscular chest that contrasted sharply with his rounded belly, had met the two at the Puerto Princesa Hotel shortly after the Four Musketeers, as the foursome called themselves when together, arrived in Palawan. The group had opted for the early flight from Manila into Puerto Princesa that put them into Palawan midmorning.

"Let's change into our suits and get some snorkeling done before lunch," David suggested when they had finished talking to the guide.

"I'm fine with the snorkeling this morning, but I have plans for this afternoon," Whitt took a sip of her coffee, one eye on her husband.

"You're not shopping again, are you?" David glanced up and shook his head slightly at his wife's proposed round of shopping therapy. He got ready to say something before Finley interrupted.

"So where did the diving guide say y'all were going to go?" Finley directed her gaze at Max, signaling him to help her change the subject before David got himself into hot water.

Max picked up the cue and described the course that had been charted for the "seafari" they were embarking on.

"We'll do the hot spots like the reefs off Puerto Princesa as well as El Nido before we head up to Coron." Max's finger sketched an imaginary route up the coast.

3

Finley pictured the map of Palawan in her mind and saw the sailboat the men had chartered following the course north and then slightly east.

"And it looks like we are going to Tubbataha!" Max concluded.

"That's a UN World Heritage Site, isn't it?" Finley asked.

David, distracted by the talk of the boating trip, answered. "Yes, and reputed to be one of the most beautiful locations in all of the Philippines, if not the world."

"It says here that the reef is part of the Tubbataha Reef Marine Park near Cagayancillo Island." Whitt had pulled out one of her many guidebooks and was reading from a page. "It's so renowned by the Philippines that they even put it on the back of their 1,000 peso note."

"Thanks for being willing to take the extra time so we could do Tubbataha. I wasn't sure we could fit it in, given the distance." David reached and took a piece of bacon from Whitt's plate, giving her a chunk of papaya in exchange.

"As if they really have to suffer, David," Max gave Finley a sly grin. "Our wives get a few extra days of massages that we agreed to pay for!"

Finley smiled. She had begun to like it now when Max called her his wife, notwithstanding their less-than-formal marital arrangement. He had taken to addressing her as such shortly after their commitment in London almost a year and a half ago.

It had gotten her in trouble, though, when he went so far as to intimate to relatives at Whitt and David's wedding in Charleston that they were married. She'd had to explain to him that in the South, skipping the big wedding, especially if you had the means, generally led to speculation about whether the bride was already with child.

Finley looked at her sister nestled in David's arms and saw the same contentment in Whitt that she felt with Max. There was a time when Whitt had sworn she would never get married. And yet now, here she was, married and very much in love.

4

"When does Charlie arrive?" Finley asked, seeing the potential tiff between David and Whitt over Whitt's shopping averted.

"Tomorrow morning. She's taking the same flight that we were on, but she's coming straight to the Summit," Whitt replied, sneaking another piece of papaya from David's plate.

"Well, I, for one, am going to take advantage of the sun this afternoon, while these ladies head out on their venture." Max angled his body closer to Finley on the banquette as he spoke. "And then I am going to recommend that we take these beautiful women out for a special dinner before we part ways. As much as I am looking forward to the time at sea, I'm going to miss my lady love."

Finley was a bit surprised by Max's sentimentality. Normally, the man was the epitome of stoicism. For the longest time, she had assumed that only she had been torn up by their parting in Tangier many years ago. Every indication was that Max had moved on after she left.

A chance meeting in Tangier a few years later revealed that nothing could have been further from the truth. Max too had been destroyed by their breakup but had shown it in ways not apparent to most. More recently, however, he had loosened his reserve and talked more openly, with deep affection. Finley had to admit that as much as she liked it, it took a little getting used to.

After they left the guys by the pool and headed to the shops, it took some time browsing to get Whitt "shopped out."

"Give me your bags, Whitt. I'll sit here while you finish. I refuse to walk anymore!" Finley sat down in the little courtyard that connected several of the shops to rest her feet after visiting the ninth store.

Finley laughed as Whitt dropped her parcels and scurried off to the next artisan's shop.

Any excuse to shop was good enough for Whitt. She had inherited Mama's shopping gene, no doubt. It didn't matter where they were in the world—Whitt was going to find the best shops and exhaust their inventory before she left. That said, she always came back with exquisite finds. Finley, on the other hand, abhorred shopping and was just as happy having Mama and Whitt as her personal shoppers.

"Did you see that?" Whitt came back and sat beside Finley on the bench. She directed her eyes toward a large entourage of people clustered around a petite, stylishly dressed woman. The woman wore a brightly patterned shirtdress that accentuated her small waist and shapely legs. Her hair was carefully coiffed into a lacquered blowout that stood firm against the ocean breeze.

Finley looked over and shrugged.

Whitt shook her head at her sister's indifference. "That's Angela Pineda. She was a former Miss International. That was almost twenty years ago, but she's revered here. Still has quite a few local endorsements."

Finley flinched when the former Miss International snapped her manicured fingers impatiently at another woman before summarily dismissing her with a flick of her wrist. The other woman moved away, apparently as told. Finley thought she saw an angry glare exchanged between the two when the woman took a seat on an empty bench a few feet away.

"You see that tall Indian guy with the Anglo chick on his arm?" Whitt was now peering over her shoulder and nodding in the direction of something behind her.

Finley glanced at the man and shrugged again.

"You are hopeless! That's Arun Mehta, the big Bollywood star."

"Should that tell me something?"

"You know, he was the lead in that movie, *Remembrance*, you saw with Max in Delhi?" Whitt tried to trigger her sister's memory before giving up and moving on.

Finley took a second look at the man, but nothing notable came to mind. She knew she was hopeless when it came to keeping up with current entertainment trends. Her taste veered more to ancient than modern culture.

"Like night and day how they're traveling." Whitt was looking at the two stars. "Arun trying to keep his head down and not be seen. And Miss International trying to attract as much attention as she can get!"

"When his star wanes, he'll probably do the same," Finley remarked after observing the two groups. She ran her eye over the rest of the crowd as they carried on with their shopping, looking for others that might be members of the glitterati. "Anyone else rich and famous that I missed?"

"None that I can see, but let's grab a glass of wine at Tomaso's and see who else we can spot. I was told that is the go-to spot for 'stargazing' on the island." Whitt gathered up her multitude of bags and started toward Main Street.

"Stars? From where?"

"Hong Kong, and occasionally the US. Who knows who we will see."

"Don't mean to be rude, but Puerto Princesa doesn't strike me as the type of place any movie star worth his salt would go."

"You wouldn't know them if you saw them! But you do have a point. Puerto Princesa is on the water, but there isn't much to see. A few hotels, a cluster or two of shops, and a sprinkling of restaurants. No five-stars that I've seen." Whitt headed toward the pier. "But who knows."

The waiter at Tomaso's showed them to an outside table tucked away on the side of the broad veranda. The table's location gave them a charmed view of the water—and the other guests, of which there were quite a few. For the first few moments after she and Whitt ordered, Finley sat back and took in the expanse of water in front of her. It was a postcard-perfect picture of the lagoon with palm trees, a stretch of beach, and a rainbow of blue water that started with deep navy before flowing into aquamarine and ending in a shocking blue green.

Finley glanced up from her water reverie at the sound of boisterous voices. Parts of Miss International's entourage, including the dismissed woman, had planted themselves at a large table in the center of the restaurant and were engaged in an animated conversation. Miss International herself, however, was nowhere to be seen.

Finley took a sip of the sauvignon blanc the waiter had just brought and raised her voice slightly to be heard over the nearby conversations. "What treatments are you going to get done at the Summit?"

"I listed out several things I want to try." Whitt scanned the crowd looking for more celebrities before glancing at the Miss International group with pressed lips and a raised brow.

Finley chuckled under her breath at her sister's reaction before continuing with the conversation. "I tried a seaweed wrap when I was in Thailand and liked it. Maybe I'll do that again."

"The diagnostic scan they do seemed pretty interesting. And some of the hydrotherapy sessions sounded relaxing." Whitt picked up an olive and popped it into her mouth, returning her attention to Finley.

"I'm going to stick to the spa and yoga options. The description of some of the other treatments verged on proctology if you ask me."

At Finley's last comment, Whitt almost spit the olive pit across the room. "You're incorrigible!"

"Well, it's true! Did you read the flyers carefully? They are talking about probing and prodding places that I'd just as soon leave alone." Finley cast a side glance at her sister.

"You have gotten risk-averse in your old age"

"And since when did you get so adventurous?"

"Since I won this trip. It's not often that you get to try this stuff out, all expenses paid." Whitt sprang to her feet. "We'd better settle our bill and get back. I almost forgot. We have dinner with the boys tonight!"

When the alarm went off at 4:00 a.m. the next morning, Finley wanted to turn over and go back to sleep. The foursome had drunk their way well into the morning. However, powered by adrenaline, Max had jumped out of bed and bolted for the shower as soon as the alarm rang. In no time, he was dressed, outfitted in a powder-blue rash shirt, navy surfer shorts, and deck shoes. He stood, bag in hand, ready to head down to grab the breakfast packs the hotel had made for them.

While he waited, Finley slowly pulled on a sundress and ran a brush through her hair before heading off to the bathroom to brush her teeth.

"This is as good as it gets," she announced as she glanced in the mirror and staggered sleepily back into the room. She leaned against the door with her eyes closed. "This is inhumane! Are you guys getting up this early every morning?"

Max walked over and pulled her away from the wall and into his arms. "My beautiful Sleeping Beauty. How I am going to miss you!"

He kissed her eyelids, her forehead, and her nose before engaging her lips with a kiss so thorough that Finley hung in Max's arms limply when they pulled apart.

"That was nice. Very nice. I think I like being missed," Finley drawled, her eyes still closed.

Max deposited her on the edge of the bed and reopened his duffel bag to throw in a few more items he had forgotten.

"That new puppy of David and Whitt's is a heartbreaker," he said as he rearranged the clothes to fit a solar charger in his Dopp kit.

"Delilah *is* cute. And the two of you got along like old pals. It was so sweet—you asleep with her curled up on your chest." Finley smiled at the image of her tall, muscular partner and the caramel handful of retriever snuggled together.

"You think our babies will do that?" Max looked up from zipping his bag closed and held Finley's eye. Lately he had been asking about babies and raising children. He was clearly signaling that he was ready. But was she?

"I think they will, when they feel safe and secure." Finley leaned up and touched his cheek gently.

When the guys departed a few minutes later for their diving trip, Whitt and Finley headed back upstairs. Their car to the Summit wouldn't arrive for another few hours.

"You headed back to bed?" Whitt asked when they reached the doors to their respective rooms.

Finley shook her head. "Nope. I was going to shower and then go get coffee out by the water."

"Good idea. I'll join you. And I'll call the resort and ask the car to come early."

Just over an hour later, a black Range Rover from the Summit pulled up in front of the hotel. The driver, an angular man with a short, spiky haircut that protruded at random angles under his uniform cap, placed their luggage in the back and helped the sisters take their seats.

"Welcome to the Summit. I am sure you will enjoy your stay. If there is anything I can get for you before we begin the short ride up the hill, please let me know. There is water in the fold-down armrest, and the international editions of *The New York Times* and *Financial Times* are in the seat pocket."

He paused to see if Finley and Whitt had any immediate needs. "If not, we will be on our way."

In no time, the bustle of the town proper was forgotten amid a forested area that ended at a stone gate, marked THE SUMMIT, which opened to a long palm-lined lane. At the end of the lane was a two-story thatched wooden edifice with pillars of stone that matched the entry gate. All around, verdant palms, interspersed among strategically placed pools, danced in the morning breeze.

The spa, set on twenty acres of manicured grounds nestled in the heart of a jungle that overlooked the sea, was opened ten years earlier to provide a health-centered oasis for those who wanted to escape the hustle of Manila but weren't into the diving focus that pervaded most visits to Palawan. In the ensuing years, it had gained a reputation as one of the most exclusive spa resorts in Asia, if not the world.

"Welcome. I hope Jun made your trip enjoyable!" A bright-faced young woman in a skirt and beautifully embroidered blouse made of sheer *pinya* fibers greeted them at a flower-strewn entrance.

"It smells so good. So restful," Whitt commented as they followed the woman inside to reception.

"Sandalwood and lemongrass. My name is Dalisay. I am here throughout your stay to ensure that it is a good one and that you come back to visit us again soon. Just a moment."

While they waited, Finley and Whitt took in the magazine-worthy view as Dalisay gathered their welcome packages. They turned in their chairs to follow the beamed ceiling as it soared into a steep raffia-lined pitch. Four large hewn trees, the supporting posts, stood like sentries at each corner.

Three of the building walls were open to the carefully sculpted landscaping. Around the floor areas, bentwood and rattan chairs, like those on which the sisters sat, were arranged in careful clusters, separated by tree-trunk tables polished to a natural sheen.

Serenity. This place oozes serenity from every pore. There is little that can disrupt something this peaceful, Finley thought as she surveyed the room.

The young woman returned ready to guide them on a tour. "Nimoy will take care of your bags while we orient you to the property and all that it has to offer. As I mentioned, my name is Dalisay, and I will be your guide throughout your stay."

Whitt and Finley nodded and fell in step beside her.

"I understand that another guest will be joining you shortly. When she arrives, we will escort her to your villa. In the meantime, let me acquaint you with the resort."

"Thank you. Her name is Charlie," Whitt offered and joined Finley for the tour of the grounds.

By the time Finley and Whitt arrived at the room after their tour, they had already signed up for an afternoon yoga class to ease them into the spa life. They took a few minutes to investigate their space: a small house with three en suite bedrooms, a spacious sitting and dining area, and a large kitchen. Two sides of the complex—those that contained the sleeping and sitting rooms—opened out onto a balcony that was suspended over a leafy ravine. On one of the remaining sides there was a small swimming pool with lounge chairs.

Finley took in her surroundings. "Okay, this is not bad. Not bad at all."

Whitt snickered before heading into her room to hang her clothes. "And it's all free!"

No sooner had the sisters unpacked their bags than they heard a faint knocking on the villa's front door.

"Charlie!" Whitt acted as the official greeter, pulling her friend into the entryway and pointing the way to Charlie's room for the porter carrying her bag. "Did you just get in?"

"About fifteen minutes ago. And then I went through the greeting ritual. You would have thought as many times as I have been here, they would have dispensed with the formalities and just brought me to the room. In any event, I'm in the same yoga class you signed up for."

"Great! We're all set for activities today," Whitt said as she watched her friend take in the setting.

Charlie walked over to the open patio terrace and breathed in. "This is what you come here for! Hear that? Silence! Absolute silence!"

A petite strawberry blonde, Charlie had been Whitt's best friend since moving to the Philippines. The director of a no-kill animal shelter, Charlie had become like a second sister since Whitt's wedding. In Charleston, she had gotten to see the sisters in action, when they worked to solve the mystery of a body found in the Airbnb in which they were staying. Now Finley watched her take in the tranquility that surrounded her, eyes closed.

She turned to give both Whitt and Finley a hug. "Now you may break my reverie. What time did you guys arrive?" she asked.

"Maybe thirty minutes before you did. The guys left at the crack of dawn, and Whitt and I lazed about with coffee on the beach until we headed up here," Finley relayed.

"Have you guys unpacked? I want a walk before I deal with that task. You up for it?" Charlie suggested.

"Suits me," Whitt replied.

"It's been a tough week, and I need to decompress, if you guys don't mind."

The sisters quickly nodded, and the threesome struck out along the manicured paths that led through the grounds.

"Looks pretty quiet. I guess it's still early, though. Most of the guests will check in tonight for the weekend," Finley observed.

"Gosh! I guess it is," Whitt checked her watch. "Only ten o'clock. The morning is still young." Whitt pointed to a sign, turning to Charlie. "Let's go to the waterfall! Do you know where it is?"

Charlie nodded and led the way. The path narrowed as they wound their way through the lush vegetation toward the falls. Fallen leaves and decaying palm fronds blackened the pebbles and coconut mulch that covered the way, lit only by periodic shards of sunlight that cut through the canopy.

They heard the rush of the water and felt the mist from the spray long before they arrived at the falls itself. As they came around a large boulder, the beauty of the falls met them full-face.

"Oh my goodness, this is spectacular!" Finley gushed, pulling her camera from her backpack and panning it across the verdant panorama, the shutter clicking the whole time.

Whitt and Charlie hung back as Finley approached the falls for some close-ups.

"Who would have thought you would have your own private falls tucked back here?" Finley moved forward, never taking her eye from the viewfinder or her finger from the shutter.

After shooting several frames, Finley shifted to look back at her sister and friend, who had ceased talking. She assumed they, like her, were silenced by the magnificent view.

"Isn't this amazing?" Finley started to say. She stopped short.

The stunned looks on the faces of Charlie and Whitt said something else.

Finley followed their line of sight and finally understood their reaction.

There, on the surface of the pool, at the foot of the falls, half hidden in the flowering vines that covered the face of the waterfall, was the form of a young woman.

At first, Finley thought she was just floating on her back. But when she failed to move after several seconds, Finley realized what Whitt and Charlie already knew.

The poor woman was dead.

2

T TOOK OVER AN HOUR before the police finally arrived at the scene. Not because they were delayed investigating another incident or were understaffed. No, the delay was caused by Summit staff who initially refused to summon the police.

"Surely, this is an unfortunate accident. Nothing that you, our esteemed guest, should worry about." The general manager, Mr. Nino Flores, an officious-looking man whose pompadoured hair made him look like an Elvis impersonator, placed a hand on Finley's shoulder in assurance.

Finley raised an eyebrow and stepped away. "This is more than an accident!"

"No need to summon the police. The young woman was one of our staff. This is an internal matter that we can handle." The manager tried to move toward the door of the small office in which he and the three women were standing.

None of the women moved.

"I hope you don't plan on moving the body without police presence." Finley held the man's eye as he continued to sidle to the door. "Tampering with evidence is a serious offense."

"You must understand. This is an affront to the reputation of the hotel. We have important guests arriving soon. There will be press. We can't have police cars blocking the entrance! We just can't!"

"Then I suggest you call them now so they can be about their business," Whitt snapped. She pointed to the landline on the desk. "Call them. Now."

The manager simpered a bit before picking up the receiver and placing the call.

In the time before the swarm of police officers arrived at the falls, Finley, Whitt, and Charlie maintained watch over the young woman's body, still afraid that the resort might spirit it away and contend that the sisters and Charlie had invented the whole thing.

"She has a uniform on, so she's resort staff. That's why the manager was trying to make it an internal matter." Finley was walking up and down the edge of the shallow pool at the foot of the falls. Periodically, she would look up toward the top of the falls. "How high do you think this waterfall is?"

Whitt moved to stand beside her sister. "Don't know. Maybe ten feet or so? Why?"

"It doesn't seem that high. I was just wondering whether the fall would be enough to kill you."

Charlie joined the conversation. "Wouldn't it also matter how deep the pool is? I mean, even if it isn't that high, if there are rocks at the bottom or it's shallow and she hit her head, she would have suffered serious injury."

"True. But wouldn't she be face down if she slipped?" Whitt asked, looking at the body staring skyward.

"Or even if she was pushed," Finley added. "Which makes this look more like murder. Like she was killed someplace else and placed here."

Those last words hung in the air. The women went silent, as if in collective prayer. They were interrupted by the sound of voices, and soon an army of police officers came into view.

A slight man with midnight-black hair and a commanding air led the pack.

"He must be the person in charge," Whitt whispered as they watched him survey the scene. The resort manager scurried behind him.

The senior officer listened as the manager tried to explain why there had been so long a delay in placing the call to the police after the discovery.

"Next time, call us immediately," the senior officer instructed.

"Next time? We can't ever have a next time or my career will be over," the manager mumbled.

The senior officer shook his head and directed his attention to the women standing vigil.

"Ladies, I am Officer Tommy Guzman. I am sorry that your stay in Palawan has been disrupted by such unpleasantness. I am hoping that we can get the information we need from you and let you be on your way. So sorry."

He motioned for a woman in uniform to come over. The young woman immediately pulled open her notebook and stood waiting for the questioning to begin.

"Can you tell me what happened?" Officer Guzman looked at the three women as they decided who would lead the responses. After a short while, Finley and Charlie both nodded at Whitt, who recounted coming to the resort and the brief walk that preceded their discovery.

The officer continued with his questions. "Had you seen the young woman before?" All three women shook their heads.

"We only just arrived a couple hours ago. You can check the registry," Finley replied as she watched the police lift the dead woman from the water. "From the looks of the body, she has been in the water for several hours."

The hotel manager who had been fidgeting with his watch, the woman officer who had been taking notes, and the senior officer in charge who was still surveying the scene stopped and turned their attention toward Finley.

"Are you a doctor or in forensics, ma'am?" Officer Guzman cocked his head to the right, making his head look like it was off the hinge.

"No, not at all. Just general knowledge—and TV shows." Finley raised her eyebrows and shrugged innocently.

I sure as hell don't want to tell him that I have been involved in previous murder investigations in at least five different countries, Finley thought. *Not something that we really should broadcast.*

"What prompted your comment, ma'am?" The officer's gaze was not challenging but rather inquiring, as if he really wanted to know the answer.

"Just something I remember about lividity, the way blood pools once the heart stops pumping it through our veins. I think it sets in after a few hours. All the blood looks like it's in the lower parts of her body, the parts that were heaviest. Like her hands, her feet," Finley explained. "But I'm sure your forensic guys know all about this stuff."

Officer Guzman shook his head and smiled wryly. "We don't have those resources. They will have to come from the city. In the meantime, important evidence may be lost."

Finley nodded. She admired his respect for the evidence. She held her camera aloft. "Would it help if I took some pictures for you to send to them while you wait for the forensics team to get out to Palawan?"

Finley remembered the pictures she had taken in Jaipur when a crime scene was at risk of being destroyed. She had been working alongside Chief Inspector Gareth Evans, an Interpol agent who had saved the sisters from trouble numerous times over the years.

Then, Evans had been undercover and powerless to intervene to preserve the scene. He had been glad that Finley was able to help save the information necessary for the police to build their case with a few frames from her camera.

"Thank you, but we do at least have a camera," Guzman teased. "If you will follow Officer De la Cruz back to reception, we will take your statements. Thank you for your assistance, and again I am sorry to interrupt your holiday."

The sisters and Charlie followed quietly behind the uniformed female officer. Mr. Flores walked beside them, muttering to himself.

After some time, he spoke, "This must be handled quickly. Angela Pineda, the former Miss International, will be arriving in just over an hour. With the press. We cannot have a scandal. It will be ruinous for the Summit, ruinous for me. I have a wife, five children, and a mother to support! This cannot happen! It simply cannot!"

The women looked at each other, unsure what to say in response.

Finley understood his predicament, but she also was well aware of the time-consuming steps involved in doing a murder investigation well. In the pit of her stomach, she suspected that, in the relative scheme of things, the arrival of Miss International would carry more weight than the investigation of a "mere staff member." She had no doubt that the police would be gone by the time Miss International and her entourage arrived.

As the threesome got closer to the reception area, Flores hurried forward and ushered them through a side entrance into a small office in which stacks of printer paper and menu folders were stored.

"Please have a seat! I hope this will work as a place to talk." The manager directed his comments at the police officer, who had dropped her notebook on the table and readied herself to take the statement. He hovered by the door, preparing for his escape. "I will have tea brought in for you."

The officer had no sooner turned her head than Flores was gone. "He's in a hurry, clearly. In any case, I will take your formal statement and then let you get back to your holiday. I am sure we will find that this was all an unfortunate accident."

It took less than ten minutes for the officer to record and then read back their collective statement. None of the details that the women provided about the position or condition of the body were captured. Finley's observations about lividity and possible time of death were skimmed over.

"They want this over. I bet it will be ruled an accident without any real investigation," Finley fumed as they left the makeshift police office.

"You're probably right, Finley, but this isn't our fight. Leave it alone. Let some other white knight come and save the day on this one. For once, let's not get involved," Whitt implored.

Finley shook her head at her sister's emphatic plea. "You really must need this rest. You normally would be on this girl's case like white on rice. Everything okay?" Finley cast a look at Charlie searching for a clue. Charlie simply shrugged.

"I don't mean to sound so cold. That poor woman is dead. It's just been a rough couple of months with work, running between Tbilisi and here, trying to find a new house, getting David oriented to Manila. I'm just spent . . . I need a break, however small, and a chance to not have to think so hard." Whitt had stopped in the lobby. The Zen-like trickling of the fountains made her words even more strident.

Finley reached out and touched her sister's shoulder, fully expecting Whitt to recoil as she often did when emotionally fraught. But this time, with the touch, Whitt exhaled and smiled sadly at her sister. She mouthed a silent "thanks" before striking off for their room. Charlie and Finley exchanged a brief querying shrug and fell in behind.

Notwithstanding the discovery of the young woman's body, all afternoon classes were on, according to the Summit staff. As expected, the resort had cleared the police out quickly and put the grounds to rights in preparation for the arrival of Angela Pineda. Uninterested in the local celebrity, Finley, Whitt, and Charlie found their way over to the fitness pavilion, where the yoga classes were to be held. Outside the studio, a small cluster of women, with a scattering of men, stood. They were a visually interesting mélange.

Finley observed the scattered crowd. Toward the edge of the cluster was what she assumed was a family—a woman in her midthirties with dark-brown hair that shone chestnut in the bright sunlight, freckles, and an athletic build; a fair-skinned man standing beside her, presumably her husband, with a slight paunch and whose hair bordered on ginger; and two preteens, a rather bookish-looking boy—a ginger, no wonder—and his sister, who was a pretty girl, likely to grow into a beauty but for her attitude, which was churlish, especially toward her parents. It was clear that neither of the children were into yoga and were only there at their parents' insistence.

Finley shifted to catch the conversation of another cluster of three women who stood talking to Whitt and Charlie.

Anywhere else and I'd say they were cheerleaders.

All three looked to be in their twenties and had the enthusiasm to match. The tallest of the trio was a wiry, dark-haired woman with what sounded to Finley like a discernably American accent. Beside her was a petite blonde. The last of the group was of average height with intense dark eyes that looked like they could curdle milk. They were currently fixed on a man in sunglasses who watched the clutch of women from one of the nearby salt pools. After watching him for a minute or so, the woman returned her attention to her friends and the conversation.

"Have you just arrived?" Finley's observations were interrupted by an older woman who stood away from the group. "I'm Noelle, Noelle Cashman." She extended her hand. Finley heard a clipped British accent in the introduction.

"Finley Blake. And that's my sister Whitt over there." Finley pointed in the general direction of where Whitt and Charlie were still engaged in a lively conversation. "And yes, my sister, our friend, and I just got here this morning. How long have you been here?" She purposely skipped over the part about the body that greeted their arrival.

"A week thus far. I normally come for a ten-day restorative. I used to come once a year, but with all the uncertainty in the market,

I find I now am coming two and three times a year," Noelle chuckled. "And who said banking was a boring business!"

"So, you're a banker—on the investment side, I take it?" Finley was intrigued now as to exactly what the woman did as a banker. Foreign exchange, equities, maybe M&A?

"Yes, commodities," the woman replied.

Finley struggled to mask her surprise.

Noelle laughed at Finley's reaction. "Yes, most people don't expect a woman to deal in soybeans, wheat, and pork bellies, but it's an exciting market and I like the pace. You never get bored."

"I would suppose not," Finley responded.

The doors to the studio were opened by a Filipino man in loose-fitting pajama-like pants and an open vest. The fifteen or so participants wandered into the studio, whose side shutters had been thrown open to the air and lush landscape, and were soon being led through the gentle stretches and poses of classical hatha yoga.

At the interval, everyone but the instructor headed for the surrounding gardens. The yoga hadn't been strenuous, but Finley and the others had begun to feel the warmth generated by the slow movements. The breeze through the palms felt good on her skin, and Finley closed her eyes to welcome it.

"Whitt says you're her sister!" Finley opened her eyes to find the tiny blonde with whom Whitt and Charlie had been speaking earlier standing in front of her. "Sorry! I forgot what she said your name was."

Finley smiled. She couldn't place the accent. It had a British tinge to it, but it came from somewhere else. Her first thought was Australia. A lot of Aussies came to Southeast Asia for holiday. But then again, the woman's slight elongation of words sounded softer than most Australians she had heard.

I guess it's like trying to place an American accent. If it's not clearly New England or southern, it's hard to determine, Finley surmised.

"I'm Finley, and yes, I'm Whitt's sister." Finley looked over at Whitt as she spoke. Whitt already seemed to be in a better mood.

The yoga had worked its magic. Finley addressed the young woman, "Where are you from? Is this your first time here?"

"So sorry, where are my manners? I'm Anya and I'm from Zimbabwe. Outside Harare to be exact," the woman replied excitedly. "Yes, this is my first time at this spa. Mark comes here all the time. Normally stays on the boat, but we needed repairs or something. So we all came up here. We're staying in the Executive Suites. Do you know which of the massages and treatments are the best? Mark says we can try any of them that we like."

Finley was still trying to figure out who Mark was when Noelle and another woman walked over.

"You seem to be pretty skilled at some of the poses our yogi is doing. Have you done a lot of yoga before?" the woman, whose accent labeled her as British, asked.

She was someone Finley had seen before, but she couldn't place where. The options were fairly limited since she and Whitt had only been here at the resort and in Puerto Princesa. In her thirties, she was slim with a mass of wavy brown hair and a welcoming demeanor.

Finley chuckled, "Hardly skilled. I think I just mimic pretty well. That's all. I don't believe we have met. I'm Finley Blake. I think you met my sister Whitt and our friend Charlie."

The woman shook the hand Finley had extended. "Melinda, Melinda Danvers. My boyfriend and I arrived last night, but this is my first class this visit. He's hanging out by the pool. We generally start slow and then work up to the serious 'medical' treatments." She used air quotes to describe the treatments.

"Anya here was just asking what treatments were worth doing." Finley turned to the little blonde with a nod in Noelle and Melinda's direction. "I think we have found our resident experts."

"Noelle and I have met here several times. Arun likes coming several times a year. We spend some time on the boat and then come in for treatments. The past couple of years, Noelle and I have been in sessions together. We luckily overlapped again this year."

Noelle nodded, "Lucky indeed!"

Melinda gently hugged her older friend. "We love the massages and wraps and any of the aqua therapies."

"And some of the detox treatments are quite good. I'm scheduled for the sensory deprivation chamber tomorrow. I keep making the same mistake my friends do, calling it the antigravity capsule. Silly me! Never tried it, but I'm looking to see how many years it takes off me!" Noelle laughed at the last comment.

"As if you need any years taken off!" Melinda rejoindered. "I was booked for the chamber tomorrow morning, but then Arun signed us up for couples massage, and I couldn't disappoint him. I'll book it later."

"Time to get back to class," Anya chirped as the instructor called them back in. "But maybe we can meet at the juice bar after class, and you can tell my friends and me which sessions we should take."

Anya looked so eager, Finley chimed in, "Yeah, it would help us make the most of the short time we have here since we are only staying through the weekend."

Noelle and Melinda were both at the juice bar in the activities pavilion by the time Finley, Whitt, and Charlie sauntered over after class. Anya and her friends were nowhere to be seen.

"Where is our little friend?" Melinda asked as Finley and the others walked up.

"She and the other girls went off with some guy that was hanging by the pool. She sent her apologies." Finley took a seat beside Noelle and introduced her to Charlie and Whitt. "I believe you know Melinda."

Introductions completed, Finley took the opportunity to find out a bit more about some of the guests at the resort. She was especially interested in Mark and the man in the dark shades who had spirited the young women away.

"Anya says this is her first time here but that some guy named Mark comes all the time. Have you guys met him?" Finley looked up from perusing the menu.

"Mark Sanderford? Yeah, we know him. Arun is supposed to meet up with him some time this weekend," Melinda replied. Seeing the confused look on the other women's faces, she continued. "He brokers yachts. My boyfriend is in the market for a boat. Tired of chartering."

"So that's it. He's rich as Croesus, and Anya and the other ladies are part of his entourage." Whitt glanced over at Anya and the other girls as they made their exit. "The guy in the glasses must be their bodyguard."

"Whatever would those girls need a bodyguard for?" Finley asked. "It felt like he was more of their keeper than protector."

"You never know. Arun usually has one when we are traveling in the cities, but when we come out here, he dispenses with protection. People can get crazy when they see celebrities," Melinda explained matter-of-factly.

It was then that it dawned on Finley where she had seen Melinda before—in Puerto Princesa in the company of the Bollywood actor Whitt had pointed out. Whitt must have known all the while and was playing it cool. Finley decided to follow suit.

Melinda was talking to Noelle now. "Speaking of small worlds, not only do I find out that our stay is overlapping, but I run into a girl I went to upper school with—Jillian Sharp. Quite a legend, she was. A computer genius of sorts. She was a few years older than me, but she used to hack into the system and change grades for her friends or anyone who would pay her."

Charlie's eyes widened. "Did she ever get caught?"

"Never! Graduated with a first and never got found out. For all her smarts, though, she was clumsy as hell. Still is."

"How so?" Charlie took a sip of the juice concoction set in front of her.

"When I introduced her to my boyfriend last week, I told the grades story to Arun and a few others who were sitting around a few days ago. She was so uncoordinated she spilled her drink on me. Stopped the conversation real quick."

"How awful! I hope she apologized," Finley said.

"It was pretty bad. Ice-cold and sticky liquid dumped in your lap. In any event, when I got back from cleaning my skirt off, she and her boyfriend had gone. Still, was a real surprise running into Jillian after all these years."

3

"**WHO DO YOU THINK DID** it?" Whitt was up, bright and early, dragging a willing Charlie but a sleep-grumpy Finley into the dining room to peruse the vegan breakfast offerings on the menu well before seven o'clock. The room was a large open-vaulted cabana with internal palm thatch. Beverage and dessert stations lined the walls, the only self-service options. For food service, uniform waiters were peppered about, pens at the ready. A waiter, whose name tag said BHOY, showed them to a table to the left of the room, nearest the gardens, and took their drinks order.

"What has you so chipper this morning?" Finley groaned, looking up through the steam from her goji berry tea. *At least it's hot. But it's also tasteless. I don't know how anyone with a functioning palate can stomach this stuff,* Finley thought.

"Earth to Finley!" Whitt was waving her hands in front of her sister's face. "What's with you today?"

"Didn't sleep well," Finley muttered.

Whitt smirked. "Missing your boo?"

"Maybe," Finley gave a half smile before bringing her attention back to the menu. "What are you guys going to have?"

"Probably the grain bowl. What about you, Charlie?"

"I've never had gluten-free tofu banana bread. I'm feeling reckless today," Charlie pointed to the item on the menu.

Finley had to laugh at Charlie feeling reckless. Charlie always colored inside the lines. Finley imagined a preschool Charlie deciding to wantonly express herself one day with a single wayward stroke of a crayon. Freedom!

"What about you?" Whitt was staring at Finley, whose gaze was roaming somewhere outside the dining room now as she again got lost in thought. "Finley! I know this is a rest-and-relaxation weekend, but we do need marginal focus to get basic things done, like breakfast"

Finley play-punched her sister. "Okay, I'm back. I want tofu shakshuka. Happy now?"

"Yes! Now we can order. The waiter's been over here three times already while you've been in your fog," Whitt retorted.

Finley shrugged sheepishly. "Really? I'm sorry. Luckily, we don't have a class we're rushing off to."

"Nope, just the salt pools. You still didn't answer my question." Whitt took a sip of her ginger tea. "Who do you think did it?"

Finley lowered her voice. "The real murder or are we playing the Murder Game?"

The latter was a childhood diversion they had created when they were younger and traveling the world with their parents. The object of the game was to connect fellow traveling companions to titillating trysts or devastating downturns that often had the sisters giggling uncontrollably at the sight of the unsuspecting guests. Mama never liked the game. Called it macabre.

"The Game. I thought we agreed we should stay out of the real one," Whitt whispered.

"Okay. Who's the victim?" Finley queried.

Charlie sat wide-eyed as the sisters concocted the scenario. Finley wasn't concerned, however. She knew that Charlie had seen the sisters at work before, when she visited them in Charleston for Whitt and David's wedding. *She probably is wondering, though, how we can so casually discuss murder at the breakfast table.*

"The woman in the blue caftan." Whitt inclined her head toward a middle-aged European-looking woman of medium height and sizable girth. "Found her dead in the pools. Had strange bands of bruising all over her body, but the murder weapon hasn't been found."

"Who found her?" Finley asked.

"One of the spa attendants. Saw her feet sticking out. Alerted the manager." Whitt bit into a slice of dragon fruit. "Police were called in, but they were baffled."

Finley shivered even though she had just taken a sip of hot goji berry tea.

"You okay?" Whitt asked, seeing Finley's reaction. Charlie too stopped mid-mouthful of banana bread to look at Finley.

"Yeah," Finley nodded. "Just a chill." After a moment she continued, "Not murder. Python from the jungle. Wrapped and ran."

Whitt stared, her mouth agape. "Boy! You got that one fast. I thought I had you stumped!"

"You guys are sick! How you come up with these situations is beyond me. David and Max sure better sleep with one eye open." Charlie shook her head. "I am *never* making you guys angry."

Whitt wrapped her arm around her friend. "You could never incur our wrath. You're just too sweet."

Finley laughed wryly. "Maybe she's the one that we should be careful of. It's the sweet ones you have to keep an eye on."

The comment came from experience. Twice now—once in Morocco and then in Jaipur—the nice guys had turned out to have a dark side that had murderous consequences.

"The Miss International crew is all here," Whitt observed, directing her gaze over Finley's shoulder. "Don't laugh, but I think Miss International's husband is nicknamed Spanky. Just like in *The Little Rascals*."

Finley shifted slightly in her chair. She could see Angela Pineda, the former Miss International, and the man who held her arm clearly now as they entered the dining room. Finley cast him as the husband. Following behind was an older couple, the woman of which was an older version of the beauty Miss International still was. Clustered around were two young women, nannies Finley presumed from the uniforms and the grip they had on the two children, both under the age of five. Another hauntingly beautiful woman with features that suggested she might be a younger sister walked behind. Hovering on the perimeter were two brutes of men with lumps in their hip pockets.

The woman at the center of all the activity was naturally petite but rose to a good five foot six with the towering platform heels she wore. They were a buff color that blended with her skin coloring, so they didn't throw off the line of the elegant outfit she had on. On the face of it a simple combination of off-white palazzo pants with an embroidered kurta-like tunic, the ensemble screamed refinement when viewed as a complete tableau with Miss International's application of makeup and accessories. She had been styled before she left her room. So beautifully styled that she held the allure of a beauty queen even a decade-plus later.

"Who's that?" While Whitt and Finley observed Miss International, Charlie's attention was elsewhere. She pointed subtly with her fork at a blond, movie-star-looking hunk who glided into the dining room just behind Miss International with a small group of people who surrounded him like cellophane.

While Miss International and her entourage were directed to a table center stage, this man chose a table off to the side, with full view of the action in the dining room but enough cover that he and his entourage were only partially visible.

"Oh, that must be Mark. The guy that Anya and those guys were talking about. He is a looker! As Granny would say, he's easy on the eyes. Very easy." Whitt strained her neck to catch a glimpse of Mark, obscured by one of the massive natural wood columns.

Finley laughed out loud at her sister's reaction. "Hold your horses! You're an old married woman now. You can't go salivating over other guys like that anymore. Your man'll get the naddies!"

"What are 'naddies'?" Charlie asked innocently as she focused on the Sanderford crew.

"The inadequates. That's what Mooney calls it when guys start feeling less than manly and start doing stupid stuff to boost their egos." Finley shook her head at the notion, thinking of their old friend.

Charlie chuckled, returning her attention to those at her table. "Leave it to Mooney."

Finley paused, going quiet as she thought of Max's struggle with his demons and the irrational behaviors that had resulted. He seemed to have them under control now.

"David knows I'm just looking!" Whitt assured. "I understand Mark and the girls, but who are the other hangers-on?"

Finley cast a quick glance over at the group. There were three other men who had filled up the seating at the main table and another two men with overextended biceps sitting at an adjacent table. They sat with their backs to the wall, scanning the room as they sipped their teas. One of the men grimaced noticeably, shaking off the objectionable taste as he placed his cup firmly on the table and pushed it away from him. It took him a minute to recover his steely glare and resume his surveillance posture.

Finley saw the other man continue to survey the room while his companion recovered. His eye stopped abruptly as he viewed the Miss International group holding court front and center. His neutral countenance transformed momentarily into an angry sneer before he relaxed his flared nostrils and continued his inspection of the room.

"Bodyguards? That's my guess. Wonder what he needs them for. I thought he sold yachts. I doubt he carries cash," Whitt speculated.

Charlie chortled at the last comment. "He would need suitcases to handle that volume of cash." She paused, her eyes getting wider. "Or a few fistfuls of diamonds."

Finley and Whitt both turned in surprise. Charlie smiled slyly. "What? What can I say? I learned from the best."

The sisters grinned and returned to their breakfast. Finley looked down at her empty plate and those of her sister and friend. "That wasn't too bad. I didn't even notice that it was tofu. Shall we go?"

The threesome rose and started for the door. They were interrupted before they reached the terrace.

"Charlie! Charlie!" It was Anya. "Come. Come over and meet everybody!"

Charlie glanced at Whitt to see if she minded before heading her mini entourage over to the alcove where Anya and the others were ensconced.

Mark looked up as they approached with an inquiring smile. "Who have you collected this time, Anya dear?"

Anya bounced over to the side of the table where he sat, her exuberance barely contained. "These are my friends. We met them in yoga. They just got here. This is Whitt and her sister Finley and their friend Charlie. Charlie likes dogs—and cats. She's a vet."

Finley suspected that, given fifteen minutes, Anya would have discovered everyone's life history and they all would be deciding where to meet for the reunion next year. She just had that kind of ability to draw the best out of people with her energy.

Mark stood to greet the new arrivals. Finley had a chance to observe him as they approached. He was an extremely attractive man, tall, almost towering, with a crop of sandy blond hair that he wore swept off his face but that still hung to brush his shoulders. His features—the strong, dominant jaw, the piercing blue eyes—suggested a Nordic background. In a movie, he would play Thor.

"Pleased to meet you. Anya has been talking all night about her newfound friends. When did you arrive?" Mark asked.

"Just yesterday," Charlie volunteered. "My friends were in Puerto Princesa for a day before arriving. I came from Manila. Anya said you are getting your boat fixed."

"Yes. We're waiting for a part, so we decided to wait here. Not a bad place to hang out." Mark glanced around. "I think you have already met the ladies. This is Efram, Danny, and Nathan, and those guys are Yuri and Tom. One big, happy, disjointed family."

"Well, very nice to meet you. We'll see you around," Whitt replied. She looked back over her shoulder at the group that had now returned to their breakfast.

"A strange lot, if you ask me," Finley muttered when they were out of earshot.

The threesome continued down the path that connected the dining room to the main therapy pavilion, the smell of lemongrass and lavender heavy in the air. The spa and therapy rooms veered off to the left while the primary swimming pool, gym, and ancillary salt floating pools were located to the right.

Today the women had decided to relax and laze by the floating pool before luxuriating with massages that afternoon. Maybe tomorrow they would try a few of the alternative therapies.

As they neared the fork in the path, they saw Noelle dressed in a swimsuit and cover-up walking toward the therapy rooms.

"Off to my decompression chamber appointment!" she threw up her hand.

The three women nodded in response, almost in unison. They assumed she meant the sensory deprivation tank that everyone had been raving about.

For another day! Finley thought as she passed her.

From the corner of her eye, Finley spied a man who looked very much like Inspector Gareth Evans, the Interpol agent, accompanied by a couple of other men in workout togs.

However convinced she was, Finley refused to raise the possibility with Whitt since in the past these Evans sightings had been a source of ridicule. Finley was saved from having to say anything, though.

Before she could speak, one of the men with Evans waved and introduced himself. "Hello, ladies. I'm Cam—Cameron, if you want to get technical—Clark, one of the instructors here. Welcome to the Summit."

He was a sculpted piece of manhood who bore a striking resemblance to a young Tom Selleck with his sculpted physique and wavy dark hair. All three of the women paused briefly to take in the full measure of the man before giving him their names. Charlie stood frozen in place behind Whitt when introductions were done.

The women stepped forward to shake hands with Cam, a guru-looking person called Ben Jaffries, and a man introduced as Thatcher Hayes, whom all three readily recognized as Gareth Evans.

So he's undercover again, Finley said to herself. *Wonder what he is up to this time. Hope we stay way clear of whatever it is.*

"When did you ladies get in?" Evans/Thatcher asked, his eyes falling first on Finley.

"Yesterday morning. We spent a day in Puerto Princesa. Then our husbands left on seafari, and we headed up here," Finley replied, returning Evans/Thatcher's glance with a wry smile.

She was sure Evans would know their husbands well, having met them in several far-off locations as recently as a few months ago when he had attended Whitt and David's wedding. But she wasn't sure of Cam and Ben's role in the ruse, so she held her tongue.

"And you?" Whitt asked. "I'm sure I have seen you before. Maybe at the Art of Living ashram in Bangalore? Or that other one in Jaipur?"

"Never been to Bangalore, and I'm a novice on the path to enlightenment. I'm hoping my advisors, Ben and Cam, can help me." He grinned at Whitt's attempt to discover his mission and started into the pavilion. "Well, enjoy your stay, ladies."

"You'd better call Max before he starts getting ideas about you and Evans again," Whitt suggested to Finley as they headed to the lounge chairs.

"You need to quit! I'm going to enjoy floating in the pool and clearing my mind of all distractions—including you!" Finley retorted as they chose their seats.

Finley chuckled at Max's previous suspicion that there was something between her and Evans. He had come to accept that the sisters were simply friends with the suave British detective, but things had been tense for a period.

Before long, the three women were enjoying the tranquil serenity of the salt relaxing pools. Charlie had migrated to the end of the pool, where she was doing standing laps. Whitt had decided to bake a little in the sun before hopping in the pool. Finley had the near end of the pool all to herself since there was no one else in the vicinity.

Finley could hear the spray of the surround hydro-pulsing showers, so she assumed there were other guests around, but nothing broke the inner peace created by the palm-hugged pool, the powder-blue sheltering sky, and the quiet lapping of the waves created by Charlie.

This is sublime, Finley thought as she flipped onto her back to take full advantage of the buoyancy.

"What the hell is that?" Whitt asked suddenly, turning toward the sound of shrill, unintelligible shrieking. "What in goodness name is going on?"

The screaming crescendoed before breaking into hysterical cries that resembled the pained yelping of an injured animal. The noises continued unabated, drawing the women out of the water and Whitt up from her chair.

Finley was the first into the pavilion. She followed the continued sobbing around the veranda to the therapy side of the building. She could hear Whitt and Charlie close behind.

In the recess that contained the sensory deprivation chamber, Noelle stood crying hysterically. The nearby attendant tried to console her. "A lot of people get claustrophobic in the chamber. There is nothing to be afraid of."

"It's not the chamber! There's something in there. Something crawling," Noelle managed between quick gulps of air.

"There is nothing there. It is just a reaction. You need to put it out of your mind. Perhaps a centering meditation," the attendant suggested, her focus on the crying woman who had calmed from hysteria to quiet sobs. She pulled Noelle closer, encouraging her to close her eyes and focus. "Let's give it a try."

Others, including Ben, Cam, and Evans/Thatcher, had come out of their therapy rooms and watched as the two women joined hands and counted into a breathing meditation. In time, Noelle's breathing slowed, and quiet was restored to the pavilion.

"There! You see! Nothing to worry about," the attendant whispered. "Open your eyes, and all will be well."

Noelle did as she was told. Slowly her eyes opened, and she exhaled.

"I'm so sorry to have created such a fu—" she started to say. Before she could finish, her eyes widened, and her gaze fixed once again on the chamber. She contorted her mouth into a tight grimace as the screaming started again.

Cam and Evans followed her fixed sight line to the chamber and moved closer to investigate. One small black spider, and then another smaller white one, crept through the open door of the chamber.

Cam pulled out his key ring and used the small flashlight that was attached to scan the inside of the darkened space. There, in the bottom, hundreds of creatures scrambled to find protection from the bright light. As he scanned the space, other spiders clung to the walls of the chamber, scurrying as the beam hit them.

"We need to close this up quickly!" Cam muttered to Evans as he grabbed the door handle and pulled it shut.

The attendant began to protest, but the look on Cam's face quickly silenced her.

"Take her to her room and get her some tea. We'll take care of this," he whispered to the attendant.

Evans met Finley's eye as he announced to the gathered crowd, "Looks like this area is going to be closed off for the time being. The rest of the services are available, though. Why don't we all go back to our activities? The staff seem to have it under control."

"**M**EET ME ON THE PATH near the Sulu Villas in thirty minutes," Evans whispered under his breath as he passed Finley on his way back to the therapy room to finish his session with Cam. His naturally hooded stare was even more intense than usual.

Finley nodded and started back to the salt pool.

Whitt sidled up to Finley as they headed back to the pool. "What is going on?" she asked.

"Don't know, but Evans wants us to meet him on the paths in a half hour." Finley cast a glance over her shoulder in the direction of the therapy rooms.

Whitt grimaced. "Maybe he'll read us in to whatever he's working on. Part of me doesn't really want to know."

Charlie chuckled. "You're going to get sucked in whatever it is, so you might as well go in with your eyes open."

Finley touched Charlie's arm gently. "This time, it isn't just us that are in it. You're in it, too."

Charlie blanched as the reality of Finley's statement sunk in.

"Well, let's at least go into it fully dressed. I need to change before we meet him. I've had enough of the pool for now." Whitt picked up her beach bag from the chair where she had left it to investigate Noelle's screams and threw it on her shoulder.

Some fifteen minutes later, the women, fitted out in leggings and running shoes, strode briskly along the walking trails, their eyes trained for any sign of Evans.

As they rounded the curve that ran between the Sulu Villas and the jungle, they spotted Evans and Cam at a nearby bench. Evans appeared to be doing bench dips while Cam eyed his stopwatch.

"I thought you'd never get here." Evans brought himself up to sit on the bench, a light layer of perspiration forming on his forehead. He eyed Cam. "How'd I do?"

Cam snickered at Evans's competitiveness, even against himself. "Better than yesterday. Two cycles of fifteen reps at six seconds each. Slowing it down is what hurts. You're going to feel it tomorrow."

"Let's walk." Evans stretched himself a bit before pointing toward the long trail through the jungle.

Finley remembered that it passed the falls where the women had found the body before continuing up into the gentle hills behind the spa facilities. She joined Evans as they turned to follow the path with Whitt and Charlie flanking Cam.

Evans set a quick run-walk pace for the first quarter mile, making conversation difficult. When he got to the cover of the jungle, he slowed to an ambling walk.

"Wanted to be sure it looked like we were really exercising. Now that we are out of earshot of anyone else, we can slow down and talk," Evans explained to Finley and Whitt, who had now moved forward to join her sister. Cam and Charlie followed behind.

"So a few things before you start asking us questions, since I know you're going to interrogate us soon enough." Finley cast a glance at Evans as they continued along the path.

He had grayed a bit more since the wedding in Charleston. Still ruggedly handsome, he was a big man, only slightly taller than Max and David but more muscularly built. His line of business required it. Although Finley and Whitt had seen more brain and very little brawn used in the times he had intervened to help them out, they knew that his size also likely acted as a deterrent to those who might have flirted with the idea of taking him on.

"Ask away," Evans responded. "Cam knows all about you."

"That was question number one. Whether he is with you or Summit staff. I guess you answered that question." Finley looked over her shoulder at Cam and Charlie, who were deep in conversation.

I've never seen Charlie talk that much, Finley observed. *Wonder what's going on.*

"Cam is his real name. We just changed his last name from Bell to Clark. He's a cyber expert, ex-British naval intelligence. We brought him on to help us out. He's been here about six weeks." Evans nodded over his shoulder at the towering man walking beside Charlie's petite frame.

Charlie looked up briefly and cast Finley a shy smile before returning to her conversation with Cam.

Evans continued, "I got in about a week ago as Thatcher Hayes, a successful businessman on a health holiday at the insistence of his doctors in the UK. The alternative therapies here are known worldwide, so it was a good cover."

"Who are you looking for or at?" Whitt asked.

Evans lowered his voice even though no one was visible. "Mark Sanderford, a yacht dealer, who also likes to trade a few other things, including arms."

"And you're tracking him?" Finley eyed Evans as he spoke.

"We found out through the chatter that he was coming out here for the winter months. He's come here before, so we thought he'd anchor offshore and come in every now and then for the spa. We didn't—and still don't—know if he is here to meet someone or just on holiday. In any case, we lucked out when his yacht broke down. That's when they brought me in."

"Are you going to buy a yacht from him to make the ruse more realistic?" Whitt joked.

"I've intimated that I might be in the market, just to start a conversation. We'll see." Evans cracked a sly smile. "Right now, I'm trying to figure out if he had any plausible connection to the banker who was in the tank today. She wasn't on my list of people to investigate for a connection."

"Is he known to be that ruthless? Like he would try to kill someone in a therapy tank? And what about the woman we found in the pool?" Finley slowed her pace as the questions unveiled more and more danger.

"I mean that woman was murdered, no doubt. Do you think Sanderford was involved?" Whitt added.

"So you're the ones that found her! I knew a body was found. A young masseuse. I hadn't figured a connection to Sanderford, but you're making me think I should keep looking." Evans shot a glance at Finley.

"He doesn't look dangerous," Finley recalled the amiable charmer they had met earlier in the day.

"Look, he doesn't keep those two goons within reach for window dressing. They are both protection and enforcers. Until we can figure out the connections, I would advise you ladies to stay clear of those two. I see that it's too late to say stay away from the rest of that entourage. You and the girls he has hanging around seem to have struck up a friendship, but just beware."

Whitt's eyes grew large. "They aren't assassins, are they? I mean, Anya is so sweet . . . or at least she seems so."

Evans chuckled. "I don't know what those women are capable of. I would just proceed with caution with any of that group."

Finley was puzzled now. She understood Sanderford's need for protection as well as the need to keep an eye on Anya and the other ladies. She actually feared for Anya with her bubbly personality. If Anya saw too much or talked too much, she would be expendable in Sanderford's world. But there were more in the entourage than those folks.

"Who are the others on his team? There're some guys that he was sitting with. Mark introduced them at breakfast. Are they his business staff? They never smile. Even more steely-eyed than his guards." Finley recalled the reserved greeting she and the others had received earlier that morning.

"You are very observant. They are his business team. Or at least that's what we are surmising. There is an accountant and some other guy whose role we haven't quite determined. And then there is Danny, the head of sales, who's been trying to butter me up."

"So what are you hoping to catch Mark on? I know yacht sales can't be illegal. Are you trying to get him running guns? I thought you were cybercrimes. Have they switched you to illegal arms dealing now?" Finley continued her line of questioning as they neared a crossroads in the walking paths.

Evans laughed. "No, I'm still working on cyber. And that's what this is. Trying to understand how Sanderford, whom we suspect is a 'cleaner,' is moving large amounts of money through the yacht-brokering operations for these less-than-savory characters. We know the money he takes as payment isn't clean, but we can't figure out how he's cleaning it."

"What's a cleaner?" Charlie had caught up to them by now.

Cam drew alongside her. "It's someone that takes other people's dirty money, payments for illegal activities."

". . . and 'launders' it. In this case, illegal arms trade," Evans interjected.

"They run it through the financial system so that it comes out clean on the other side," Cam explained.

"We've done a forensic scan of everything we can get our hands on, but there's nothing unusual. His books look straight, maybe too straight," Evans added.

Finley was puzzled. "But you can't convict a man for being tidy, can you?"

"We've been working on this for almost a year. I was brought in recently to see how close I could get to a real transaction." Evans paused to contemplate which of the paths he thought the group should take.

Finley was glad he opted for one other than the one that led to the falls. That area still creeped her out. Charlie and Whitt had suggested walking to the falls before breakfast, but Finley had begged off.

"Do you mind if we go through the other guests to see what you know?" Evans asked as they resumed their walk through a less dense part of the surrounding jungle.

The sisters knew it was pointless to argue ignorance. Evans would keep probing until he found a tidbit of information, something almost forgotten, that would spark his thinking. The easiest thing was to play along. Besides, it was fun. A little like the Murder Game. *Let the game begin.*

"What do you know about the banker?" Evans asked.

"Not too much. Noelle Cashman. She seems nice enough," Finley began. "I think she comes here a lot. She and Melinda remembered each other from a previous stay, I think."

Evans interrupted. "Who's Melinda?"

"She's Arun Mehta's' girlfriend. You know, the Bollywood actor," Whitt responded.

Evans and Cam both nodded.

Finley was sure they had background information on everyone currently registered at the Summit as well as those who had checked out in the last several weeks. If she knew anything about Evans, it was that he was thorough.

"Continue with Noelle, if you don't mind." Evans brought them back to the topic under consideration.

Finley and Whitt both knew it was Evans's practice to ask questions he already knew the answer to, just to be sure he hadn't missed a thread that might lead to a solution. Finley filled him in on what little she knew—that Noelle Cashman was a British banker now living in Singapore who came to the Summit periodically to decompress.

"She's single, has a cat, hates dogs, and likes her whisky neat. Besides that, not sure there is much I can tell you," Finley concluded.

"Was there anyone else here she was social with? Besides Melinda, whom you've already mentioned," Evans inquired. "I'm trying to find a connection to Sanderford."

Finley and Whitt looked at each other and shook their heads.

Evans's lips pursed and twisted as he thought. "Who else have you ladies met that you thought was noteworthy?"

Finley looked at her sister again and shrugged. "You have to understand, we just got here yesterday. In that time, we have discovered a body and seen a guest have a less than pleasant experience in the sensory deprivation tank. I think that was enough to distract us from any other observations."

Whitt paused in the middle of the path so abruptly that Charlie, who was engrossed in a conversation with Cam, almost tripped over her.

"Sorry, Charlie. Didn't mean to trip you." Whitt quickly shifted her attention from Charlie to Evans. "Do you think the death of that poor girl and the chaos at the tank were intentional—to get people looking anywhere else than at what they were doing?"

"But what are they doing?" Finley asked. "We don't know that the young girl was even known to Sanderford and his crew, and he and his entourage were still at breakfast when Noelle went to get into the tank."

Whitt's shoulders sank. "You're right. Just a thought."

"And not a bad one. There may be some sleight of hand and distraction going on. Just keep your eyes open, and let us know if you see anything." Evans smiled at the suggestion.

Finley figured he was regretting having thrown the door open to the sisters and their friend investigating. The sisters tended to find trouble, whether or not they were looking for it; Evans had seen that firsthand more than once. *He must be pretty desperate for information to encourage our participation*, Finley figured.

"Shall we sit for a moment?" Evans suggested. They had come upon a pagoda slightly off the path that had wooden benches skirting its edges. Clearly, Evans wanted to have a conclave.

"I'll be honest with you. We're coming up with little and are running short on time. As much as I normally would tell you to just go have a nice, relaxing weekend, I need eyes in multiple places, and there is only so much Cam and I can cover," Evans shared.

He continued, "If we aggregate what we know, we might be able to come up with options faster."

Just as they settled into the pagoda, a man with a long hook wrapped in what looked like black tubing walked by. He nodded to the group as he made his way down a path that led through the jungle.

"Did you see that?" Cam asked as the man passed.

"Yes, I saw the man. Was there something unusual about him?" Finley asked.

"You didn't see the python? That guy, Joseph, is the snake handler. And he was carrying a rather large python."

"Python? From where?" Whitt asked, her eyes searching the surrounding trees and ground for signs of slithering.

"We *are* in the middle of a jungle, you know. They sometimes get in. They like warm places," Evans noted.

"Just as long as they don't creep into my room." Finley eyed the snake handler cautiously as he continued into the jungle with his pole held aloft.

"Sorry for the distraction," Cam apologized. "We were talking about the money laundering and our need for evidence."

"But we don't know anything about money laundering or how it's done. I mean you had to define for us what a cleaner was!" Whitt exclaimed. "And we know even less about advanced technology."

Evans chortled at Whitt's description of their capabilities. "Maybe, but I also know that whatever situation you ladies are in, you manage with wit and a bit of cunning to navigate your way through. I need your smarts now if we're going to ferret out Sanderford's methods."

Cam glanced over at Charlie as he spoke. "Evans and I will take care of the heavy lifting. What we need are your eyes and ears."

Evans nodded and picked up on the earlier thread. "Can we finish going through each of the people you have met, what you know about them, and how they might be connected?"

"Okay. You know all that we know about Noelle and the Sanderford entourage. We haven't run into anyone from the Miss International horde, except at a distance. We'll let Whitt make that acquaintance," Finley recounted. "Charlie has talked to Lilith, the mom of the British family that is here."

"They actually aren't really English. She's fifth-generation Malaysian planter family, and he's fourth-generation Hong Kong," Charlie clarified.

"I've never met someone that's white and lived in Asia that long. It's like longtime white Kenyans who protest when people say they really aren't African because they aren't black. Africa's been their home for generations; they don't know anywhere else," Finley interjected.

Charlie continued sharing what she knew of Lilith and Jamie Anderson and their two kids, Naomi, twelve, and Eric, fourteen. Whitt jumped in to add what she knew about Melinda and Arun and to relay what Melinda had told her about her former classmate Jillian. "Strange woman, it seems. We haven't met her yet. And I am really not looking forward to that encounter."

"You'll be fine as long as she doesn't have a drink in her hand," Evans joked.

Finley turned to Evans. "The only one we're clueless about is Ben. Is he one of yours?"

At the last comment, she inclined her head toward the two men to suggest that Ben might be like them, an operative.

Cam sputtered before breaking into peals of laughter. "Ben? Ben? The man is stoned most of the time!"

"That could all be an act. People talk if they think someone is out of their head. You could gather a lot of info that way," Whitt offered.

"You have a point, but no, Ben doesn't work with us. He is a yoga nomad. A hippie in the truest sense of the word!" Evans explained as they rose to continue along the path. "And he really is stoned. But I will ask him what he knows. You can never tell."

"Back where we started." Evans had brought them back to the paths near the Sulu Villas. "Thanks for the walk, ladies. A pleasure talking with you."

Evans had slipped back into Thatcher Hayes mode. But not completely. As he turned to head to his villa, Evans issued a directive under his breath. "Ladies, thanks, but stay out of this one. Observe but do not engage. It's very dangerous."

5

WHEN FINLEY CHECKED HER WATCH, she realized that the walk along the paths with Evans and Cam had taken over two hours. While it was still scarcely noon, the threesome had worked up an appetite.

"Let's just go to lunch early. I doubt they have any snacks that are going to take the edge off this hunger." Whitt was rummaging around in her bag for nuts or Oreos or something that would satisfy her craving.

"Fine with me. I'm not that hungry, although I could do with a cup of coffee." Finley watched her sister continue to turn her beach bag inside out looking for a hidden snack.

Like phones and other electronics, outside snacks were discouraged by the Summit to allow better adherence to a healthy, relaxed regimen. Bowls of seeds and plates of tropical fruits were available throughout the resort, but those clearly weren't what Whitt had in mind.

"Well, if I can't have my shortbread, you can't have your coffee!" Whitt countered.

"I suspect you will find a pack of shortbread cookies in your backpack or one of the other bags you brought. I, on the other hand, can only dream of coffee until we head down the hill on Wednesday," Finley replied. "We'll survive. It is only a few days. Charlie, you okay with an early lunch? When we finish, we can pick up where we left off at the pools before we get our massages."

Charlie nodded and led the way to the dining room. The area was more crowded than it had been at breakfast. Tables and chairs had been set up outside the dining pavilion, scattered around the garden setting that encircled it. Finley suspected that the mass of guests they were seeing was a convergence of the early risers who were now ready for the second infusion of sustenance and those who had slept in and were just getting food for the first time.

"Where do you want to sit?" Charlie looked back at Whitt to see if she had a preference. Whitt pointed at a table centered on the side wall with a good view of the room.

The Miss International crowd had taken the alcove Sanderford had occupied at breakfast, laying claim to all five of the tables there rather than just the two that the breakfast crew had used. Angela, her husband, and the older couple sat around the larger table with the younger sister. The bodyguards took over two tables just off to the left. They too all sat with their backs to the wall, scanning the room. The nannies and the children moved to the two tables furthest removed from the activity of the main room. It appeared that one table was for eating and the other for activities.

While one nanny arranged place mats and utensils for the children so they could eat once their food was served, the other engaged the children in coloring and blocks. While complimenting the little girl, who was no older than four or five, on her choice of colors, the young woman who attended them helped the boy, about two, with stacking blocks and knocking them down.

"This is not a place that I would bring my kids, if I had any. They look so bored." Finley was observing the children, who seemed to be going through the motions of playing out of routine.

"I was thinking of the snake handler we saw earlier. The thought of pythons and little kids scares me. If they aren't on a very short leash, they can easily end up as a snake snack!" Whitt chuckled at the alliteration.

Finley and Charlie drew back in horror. "What a ghastly image! Python belly bulging with a toddler's tiny body inside."

"Or coiled around its little body so that only the feet stick out," Whitt continued.

"Stop, before I'm completely put off my lunch before I even order," Charlie begged good-naturedly.

Finley shook her head at the images Whitt described, but when she looked over at the children, she could readily see how it might happen. She had assumed that the children belonged to Miss International and her husband, but it was the younger sister who was greeted with "Mama" when she came over. She kissed the little girl's head before picking up the boy and placing him on her lap as he concentrated on his tower building.

"What are you thinking of having?" Charlie asked, her eyes still scanning the menu. "I don't want anything too heavy. All that kneading and patting this afternoon is going to be uncomfortable on a full stomach."

Whitt frowned. "I hadn't thought of that Now that you say it, maybe an early lunch wasn't a good idea."

"By the time we head to our massages, we will have digested a good portion of our lunch, I'm sure," Finley conjectured. "In fact, given that this is all veggies, we'll be ready for another meal by that time. I know David would be."

Whitt laughed at her sister's last comment. David, Whitt's husband, was known for his ability to eat large amounts of food several times a day and still be looking for more. And yet, he maintained a Mr. Universe–worthy six-pack.

"I think I am going to try one of the salads." Whitt used her finger to track the differences in the greens and condiments between the salad descriptions. "This pseudo-Greek one looks pretty good. I know the feta is going to be tofu in disguise, but who cares."

"I was looking at that one, too," Finley declared as she closed her menu.

As she looked up, she caught the eye of Melinda and a man she recalled as being Arun, her boyfriend. The couple was looking for a place to sit among the tables that had quickly filled up since Finley and her crew arrived.

"Melinda, you're welcome to join us! Looks like it's gotten pretty crowded in here," Finley offered.

While her invitation was motivated by an urge to help, she also wanted to find out more about Arun and his dealings with Mark. Melinda had mentioned his interest in buying a boat. Was this a transaction that Evans could track?

Upon hearing Finley's offer, Melinda paused and looked over at her boyfriend, who shrugged obligingly. The two walked over to the table and took their seats opposite Finley and Charlie while Whitt presided at the head of the table.

"Ladies, this is Arun. Arun, this is Whitt, Charlie, and Finley." Melinda nodded at each of the women as she said their name.

"Pleasure to meet you, as if you need any introduction," Whitt responded. "My sister and I have spent some time in India, so we are great fans of your movies."

Finley smiled at the fact that Whitt had completely overlooked Finley's cluelessness as to who was who in the entertainment industry.

"You flatter me." The actor lowered his eyes and nodded in humble appreciation of the comment.

For a man whose livelihood depended on self-promotion and a degree of hubris, Arun spent much of the conversation extolling the talents of his fellow actors and the directors with whom he'd had the pleasure to work.

"Arun is working on his first American film now," Melinda shared.

Arun beamed at the comment. "It is something different for me. My Bollywood fans probably aren't going to recognize me, which I rather like."

Whitt and Charlie leaned forward, clearly intrigued. "What is it about? Can you say?" Charlie inquired.

"We start filming next month. It is actually a comedy. I have never done one before—unless you consider all Bollywood films to be parodies or comedies, which some do," Arun answered.

"Who else is in it?" Finley wondered who she might recognize, given her limited exposure to current Hollywood or Bollywood celebrities.

"Jackie Chan!" Arun's face exploded with excitement. "He is one of my all-time favorites. When my agent said he was the headliner, I nearly fell out of my chair."

"Really! He literally almost fell over," Melinda exclaimed, touching his arm as she recalled the event. "He was on his mobile in the kitchen, having a normal conversation with his agent. And then he stops, bug-eyed, in the middle of the hallway, pulls the phone from his ear, and stares at it. I could hear Dev, his agent, talking away. And all Arun is doing is staring."

"Well, what would you do if you were told you were going to get to work with one of your idols?" Arun looked around the table. He genuinely was curious about the answers. He turned to Charlie first. "Who's your all-time favorite actor or celebrity?"

Charlie paused to think about her response. "Jane Goodall. Not really a celebrity, but I would think I had gone to heaven if I had a chance to work with her."

"So imagine someone calls and says, 'Ms. Goodall has asked whether you would consider working with her on a project.' I don't know your area of expertise, but I imagine you would be quite surprised."

"Surprised. I would probably faint!" Charlie shared.

"Now you understand my reaction." Arun laughed, his attention still directed at Charlie. "By the way, what do you do?"

Charlie explained her line of work as a vet, mainly for shelter animals, in Manila. "I recently opened a small branch operation just outside Manila with the aim of promoting no-kill shelters, but I wasn't prepared for the volume of stray animals in that area that we have had to treat."

Arun listened with interest. After a while, he touched her arm gently. "It won't solve all your problems, but it might help. I'd like to make a donation."

Charlie drew back apologetically. "Thank you very much, but I wasn't asking for you to make a contribution."

"I know. That's why I felt compelled to make one." Arun smiled.

Melinda laughed. "I have seen this man look stone-faced while someone is pitching him for money for some project or another and tell the person no. And then five minutes later, he'll call his manager and arrange a contribution to some cause or other. He gives when you don't ask, not when you do."

"Well, thank you. Sincerely." Charlie sat, hand over her heart, still in shock over Arun's unexpected offer.

"That's quite generous!" Whitt agreed. "What are you two doing this afternoon for treatments? I think you had massages earlier today. How were they?"

"Very good. It was a couples massage, so just being together was nice. I'm glad we had finished before all the craziness started," Arun said.

Melinda joined in. "Yes. What was all that? It was pretty much over by the time we got dressed and got to the veranda."

"One of the guests—in fact, it was Noelle—found crawly things in the sensory deprivation tank." Whitt shuttered just saying the words.

"They had to close it. I guess they got in somehow, and no one checked it before she stepped in." Finley was still wondering how that many spiders had entered the tank with no one noticing.

Melinda was wide-eyed. "That's horrible! I will have to go find her and see how she is doing." She looked over at Arun. "You saved me. I had originally booked that time slot. I would have died of fright."

Arun patted her hand before explaining to Whitt and the crew, "Melinda is deathly afraid of spiders. And with her heart condition, it might have had dire consequences."

"Good gracious! You were indeed lucky," Whitt exclaimed.

Arun kissed Melinda's forehead. "But no harm was done. You are quite fine, my dear."

"But just the thought terrifies me. I think I will stick to things in wide-open spaces where I can see what's coming. Poor Noelle!" Melinda's brows knitted in concern. "Maybe we should just go back to the boat."

Arun shook his head. "Sweetheart, you are overreacting. Let's enjoy the facilities for another day or two, and then we can head back to the boat."

Melinda went quiet, but she didn't seem convinced. Finley decided to take advantage of the lull in conversation to switch the topic to boats.

"So you are like Mr. Sanderford and anchor offshore to use the Summit services?" Finley asked.

Arun seemed happy to divert the conversation and calm Melinda.

"Yes. We come down a couple times a year. But this is the first time we've chartered a boat," Arun declared.

"Arun is in the market for something we can use for ocean voyages, and Mark's name came up among some friends of ours." Melinda's shoulders had dropped, and she smiled as she spoke, the concern over the near miss in the sensory deprivation tank forgotten.

"I reached out, and Mark suggested the charter this year to test it out, decide what features we like." Arun looked over at his girlfriend. "We've rather liked it, haven't we, my dear?"

Melinda nodded. "I do. I especially like the size of this one. Not too over the top, if you know what I mean."

Finley didn't, but she bobbed her head anyway. She hadn't heard much of anything from Anya and the other women about

Sanderford's yacht, but she figured it would have all the latest bells and whistles to promote sales, if nothing else. *It's worth a try to see how well they know Sanderford,* she thought.

"Have you been on Sanderford's boat? I heard it is something else."

"I haven't been on it, but we can see it not far from where we anchored. It's huge, with sonar and everything," Arun exclaimed before turning to Melinda. "I guess we are going to have to get sonar on ours if we want to do long trips."

"You and your gadgets." Melinda chuckled as the group's food arrived and everyone settled into their meals.

As she and Arun headed back to their room after lunch, Melinda extended an invitation to the table. "You'll have to come out to the boat for drinks before you head back to Manila. Maybe after your husbands get back. We'd love to meet them!"

"That is most kind. We'd love to!" Finley accepted the invitation, hoping that by that time Sanderford wouldn't have left. It might offer Evans and Cam the opportunity they needed—short of buying a yacht themselves—to get close enough to Sanderford to figure out what he might be up to. She would have to figure out how to coax Max into helping Evans, but she was sure she and Whitt could think of something.

Finley thought of what Arun's yacht might look like. She had been on a high-end private jet, courtesy of Logan Reynolds, her very wealthy friend from New York, but she had never been on a superyacht. And she imagined Mark would have leased Arun one of the best in order to get him to add the luxury upgrades to his order that he and Melinda would have gotten used to during the monthlong charter. Any smart marketer would have.

"That was fun!" Whitt declared as the crew walked toward the floating pools. "Arun is a really great guy. I wouldn't have expected it, him being a celebrity and all."

Charlie concurred. "You see him in the movie ads, and he has that arrogant look about him. So when he sat down, I was expecting to have to try really hard not to trip over his exaggerated ego. But he was just the opposite. Guess you shouldn't judge."

Whitt turned to Charlie. "How much do you think he's going to give you?" Her curiosity was killing her.

"Anything is a dollar more than we had," Charlie chortled. "I have learned not to look gift horses in the mouth and to be glad for every penny promised and surprised when the promises are actually paid."

"You have a point there—pledging and delivering the goods are two different things." Finley angled her lounge chair to better catch full sun before finally sitting down. "Now for some de-stressing time before our massages."

She had only half closed her eyes when she saw Cam walking across the grounds with Mark Sanderford. They were deep in conversation, and Mark looked none too pleased. As the two reached a fork in the path, Cam diverted his attention away from Mark and toward the pools. Cam smiled and threw up his hand. Before Finley could return his greeting, she caught motion out of the side of her eye. Charlie was waving with a shy grin on her face.

Well, I'll be. She likes him! And better yet, he likes her! Finley thought as she drifted off.

"Wake up, Sleeping Beauty. We'd better get going." Whitt roused Finley from a deep sleep a short time later. "You seem to be sleeping better out here than you do in your room at night. We need to head to our massages."

Finley stretched. "How long was I out for?"

"Only about fifteen or twenty minutes, but you were down for the count," Whitt kidded her sister. "You would have still been here asleep at dinnertime if we hadn't gotten you up."

Finley gently touched her face to check for sunburn. "I'm not burnt, thank goodness. A massage on blistered skin would not be fun."

Charlie giggled and nodded. "At least you don't snore!"

"But I do. At least I think I do once I get into a deep sleep. I suspect Max has been too polite to confirm my suspicions." Finley folded her towel and gathered her satchel. "I will now continue my nap on the hot stone table!"

The threesome was joking and laughing so much as they walked along the veranda to their massage appointments that they were almost past the yoga studio and entering the spa when Charlie stopped dead in her tracks, a look of supreme surprise on her face.

"Charlie, what is it?" Whitt was surveying the area quickly, looking for a spider or even a snake, given the degree of shock in Charlie's expression. "Is it something crawly? Where? Point it out so we don't walk up on it."

Charlie shook her head and took five or six steps back. "There!" she mouthed, turning her eyes toward the yoga studio.

The door was open just enough to see two people on the mats in the darkened studio. They were too engrossed in each other to know that anyone else was there. It was Lilith and Ben, her cow pose meeting his reclining hero's stance.

6

FOR A RESORT THAT WAS noted for its Zen, dinner at the Summit that evening turned out to be a riotous affair. The room was humming with a volume of activity and noise Finley hadn't seen before. Granted it was a Saturday night, but even so, the three women were not expecting the crowd of people that flooded the dining room.

Additional seating had been set up on the veranda and lawn surrounding the main dining room in addition to the garden tables. It was there that the threesome sat. The location gave them only a partial view of the guests inside the eating pavilion, but it was still intriguing.

"Miss International is front and center—again." Whitt spied Angela Pineda holding court with her white teacup Pomeranian on her lap as they took their seats. A small coterie of admirers gathered around her, and she was all smiles.

"Her sister looks none too happy, though." Charlie cast an eye over at the woman who sat quietly at the end of the table with her lips pressed together tightly.

"Do you think she's bothered by all the attention or the fact that none of it's coming her way?" Finley asked as she considered the dynamic among the group.

The nannies and children had been shunted over to a table along the side wall across from where Angela's sister had taken refuge. The children's space had again been divided into eating and activities. The bodyguards were now standing, back to the wall, nearby. It looked like a scene from a *Godfather* movie.

"I guess those guys'll have to eat later this time," Finley observed as she, Whitt, and Charlie waited for their server.

As she scanned the room, she noticed one of the men in black from Sanderford's team enter the room, visibly staring at the Miss International table. At first, thinking he was a fan, Finley expected to see the response to the man's stare come from Miss International herself. Then, Finley remembered that the Sanderford bodyguard was the same one who had reacted earlier to someone in the Miss International entourage. Finley watched as one of her bodyguards stepped forward to meet the Sanderford man's stare with a menacing glare. Sanderford's man smirked almost imperceptibly, turned, and left.

"Guess so. Goodness, this place is crowded. I didn't know there were this many guests on the property," Whitt exclaimed, breaking Finley's concentration.

When Finley returned her attention to the Pineda bodyguard, he was again expressionless, standing statue-still in his position against the wall.

"The size of this place is deceiving." Charlie assessed the crowd. "There are a lot of small bungalows near the Sulu cluster. I think women come down from Manila with their friends during the weekend for treatments."

"Could they make weekends silent?" Finley covered one ear to block out some of the din coming from the inside dining room. "I'm glad we are out here with the birds."

"And the mosquitoes!" Whitt slapped at her arms.

"Want another coil?" Finley offered her sister and Charlie another of the citronella-scented bracelets that helped to ward off the flying insects.

"Thanks." Whitt reached for one and quickly put it on. "Did you see Anya and her gang in there? I didn't get a good look before we came out here."

"I just saw one of the bodyguards, but I don't think any of the others are here," Finley noted.

Charlie shook her head. "I didn't see them either. They may have opted for dinner in their suite. Anya said they have several rooms together with a common living and eating area, so I imagine they just had dinner brought in."

"That would make sense with a group that large. I guess Miss International didn't get that memo—or she missed her fans too much to stay holed up in her rooms," Finley joked.

Whitt looked over at her sister, head inclined. "You don't like her, do you?"

Finley had to think about that for a moment. She didn't know the woman and had only seen her in public settings. Angela might be a completely different person when the cameras weren't rolling. Finley doubted it, though.

"I have no basis for like or dislike." Finley raised an eyebrow and gave her sister a sardonic smile. "That said, I doubt she and I could ever be friends."

Charlie chuckled. "I'm with you. Melinda and Arun are more my style of rich folks."

"What about Lilith?" Whitt's lip quirked up slightly as her eyes followed the Anderson family as they entered the dining area. Given what they had seen earlier in the day, the threesome wondered how Lilith and Ben would react to each other in public.

Lilith and her husband with the kids in tow were led to a table toward the front of the space. In getting there, she passed close to the table where Ben and another guest were dining. Ben looked up and nodded. Jamie, Lilith's husband, returned his greeting. Lilith stared straight ahead, directing her attention instead to getting the children seated.

"Ouch! Talk about a hit and run." Whitt snickered. "Did she just ignore him?"

"Yep. I could say something rude, but I think I'll keep that thought to myself." Finley took a mouthful of the stuffed squash that had been put in front of her.

Charlie had opted for a vegan lasagna that used cauliflower noodles, and Whitt had settled on a veggie stir-fry with brown rice. They all shifted their focus to their meals.

"This is excellent! Who knew you could get so much flavor from vegetables!" Whitt looked over at Charlie, who had been vegan for years, and laughed. "I guess Charlie did."

"Has anyone seen Noelle since this morning?" Finley inquired as she surveyed the room for evidence of the older woman.

"No, I guess she's still recovering. That was quite a scare she took. I'm still wondering what happened," Whitt pondered. "I mean, was it really an accident, or was someone trying to scare her to death?"

"I doubt you could really die from arachnophobia, but even if you could, who would be after Noelle?" Finley finished putting a forkful of food in her mouth and sat back thinking. She swallowed and continued, "Evans said she wasn't on their list. So what's the connection?"

"Did Evans say who *was* on the list?" Charlie probed. "I couldn't hear all that he was saying."

"You couldn't hear, or you got distracted—by Cam?" Finley teased. "You two seemed to be enjoying your conversation."

Charlie blushed. "He's a really interesting person. He did classics at Oxford. And he has two street dogs that he adopted."

Finley touched her friend's shoulder gently. "We're just teasing you. We're glad that you and Cam have hit it off."

"Oh, it's nothing like that," Charlie blustered. "We were just talking. He's working."

"Nothing says you can't see him again when you're both back in Manila, does it?" Whitt put the last forkful of her stir-fry in her mouth and raised a questioning brow.

Charlie went quiet. Whitt was always on the lookout for a cute guy for her best friend, and here this one had practically fallen in Charlie's lap. Finley knew that Whitt wasn't going to let him slip away before Charlie gave it a chance.

"Anyone up for dessert?" Whitt asked.

"I ate far too much already." Finley patted her belly. "I would love a cup of coffee, though."

"You are going to have to settle for tea. Two more days and then you can get your cup of joe," Whitt reminded her.

Finley laughed. She knew that before she saw Max, she was going to go find coffee. In fact, Max's best interests would be better served if she did.

"Then shall we head to the lounge and see what special infusions they have this evening?" Whitt suggested, pushing her chair back from the table.

They had just settled themselves in some chairs in the lobby lounge area when Whitt heard her name.

"Whitt. Whitt Blake?" The voice wasn't one she readily recognized. It was low and soft, slightly unsure.

When she turned around, Whitt recognized the man saying her name even less than she did the voice. She tilted her head in response, trying to make some connection with the man and her past, but none came. It was Charlie who connected the dots.

"Hunter?" Charlie was up from her chair and had thrown her arms around the man in front of them. "I didn't know you were still in the Philippines. I thought you had gone to London!"

The man tightened his embrace so that Charlie was almost off the ground. When he released her, he stepped back to take her in.

"Charlie! Good gracious! Aren't you a surprise! How long has it been? Four? Five years?"

Finley stood watching the recognition come to Whitt's face. This was Hunter Langley, the Aussie guy Whitt was going out with when Finley came back from Morocco the first time. Hunter had been Whitt's first serious love. They had gone out for almost a year before things started to unravel. Whitt had moved on, but it had taken Hunter a little longer to cut the ties.

"Hunter, how are you?" Whitt approached the man and kissed him on both cheeks.

Hunter tentatively slipped his arm around her waist when he returned the kiss. For a moment, he kept it there. "It has been a very long time. You're looking well."

"Where are you based now?" Whitt asked.

"Back in Manila, still with WHO. I left for a couple of years but couldn't settle into the London lifestyle, so I got another assignment out here. Been in Manila for a year now. What about you?"

Whitt and Charlie were standing to one side of the man so that Finley could look at him without staring. Only a half inch taller than Whitt with dark, almost black hair and equally dark eyes, he was much more reserved than Finley had imagined when Whitt had described him those many years ago.

Even more surprising, he sported a beard. *I thought Whitt said she would never kiss a man with a beard. What gives? Maybe that's why she never brought him home!* By the time Daddy and Mama had gotten out to visit her, Whitt and Hunter had split, and neither Mama nor Finley had ever gotten the chance to size him up.

Mama would've been surprised. She never would have picked him out as being anyone Whitt would have been interested in. Who knew! Finley chuckled to herself.

Off to the other side of Hunter stood a woman, whom Finley presumed to be his girlfriend. She too had dark hair, stylishly cut into a wavy French bob, and dark-rimmed round glasses. Against the tropical backdrop, where other guests had opted for bright, bold colors, this woman seemed given to black clothes that threw off a magazine-publisher chic. The result was that your eye was immediately drawn to her. If she was using black to make herself invisible, it wasn't working.

Charlie and Whitt were in the process of catching Hunter up on the last five years of both their lives, even as they peppered him with questions. In the meantime, the woman, who had started by observing the conversation in a relaxed mode, was getting more and more antsy. She checked her watch a few times and shifted her weight to lean into Hunter more, perhaps trying to catch his eye.

"Are you still playing?" Charlie asked.

She and Hunter had been members of a blues band called the Raiders in which Hunter played bass. Charlie still led the group on vocals and lead guitar. When she was behind a guitar, shy, reserved Charlie became a foot-stomping mix of Janis Joplin and Bonnie Raitt, with a sultry blues growl that got people on their feet.

"Not as much as I would like," Hunter's voice grew nostalgically soft.

"You should come back and join us. Same place, same rehearsal schedule. If nothing else, stop in and jam," Charlie offered.

The mention of music seemed to remind Hunter that the woman was there. He reached over and took her hand, pulling her into their conversation.

"Where's my head? Jilly, these are some of my mates from the band that I used to hang with when I was here before. Charlie, Whitt, this is my girlfriend, Jillian."

The name Jillian brought Finley to attention. Was this the woman that Melinda had mentioned? She didn't seem like the goofy, clumsy tech geek that Finley had imagined when Melinda told the grades story. Jillian was a fairly common English name. Perhaps it was someone else.

"Finley, come over and meet someone." Whitt was motioning Finley to come stand beside her. As Finley approached, her sister made the introductions.

"Finley, this is Hunter Langley and his girlfriend, Jillian. He was one of the members of Charlie's band when I first came to

Manila. He's at WHO," Whitt explained, neglecting any mention of her previous relationship with Hunter.

Finley shook hands and then turned to Jillian. "And are you at WHO as well?"

Jillian gave her a slight nod and smiled. "Yes, we both are in the informatics department there." Her accent was public school English. As Mooney would say, she was "posh," with a countenance that suggested disinterested interest. "And what do you do?"

Whitt answered for her. "Finley is a travel writer. She's actually working on a story, and Charlie and I came because of a charity raffle I won. Do you guys come here often?"

"Jilly and I came down a couple of times earlier this year on some coupons she found. And now she's used a small inheritance to allow us a little getaway." Hunter pulled the woman closer as he spoke.

He glanced casually at the women's hands. He appeared surprised when he saw the sizeable stone and simple band on Whitt's ring finger. Whitt saw the confused reaction.

"Our husbands are off diving. David and I might come back for a long weekend, but he needed to get the diving itch scratched first," Whitt relayed. Hunter's shoulders visibly relaxed, but his eyes never left her finger.

"Hunter, we probably need to head out." Jillian tapped the face of her watch. "We need to set things up."

Hunter took her hand and kissed it before proudly explaining, "Jilly is a gamer. A serious gamer in those multiplayer marathon games that are played around the world. I don't really understand them, but she is pretty highly ranked."

"He understands them enough to set them up for me. Which is pretty complicated." Jillian looked up at him and smiled. "And he knows it takes a while to connect everything."

"How do those things work?" Finley was curious. "I've heard there can be thousands of people playing. And you can actually make money doing it."

Jillian laughed. "It's like playing by yourself. You sign in and you play, but there are other people playing too with their own agendas. So they're attempting to defeat you, or you can join forces with others to defeat someone else whom you don't like. And yes, gaming is a multibillion-dollar industry, and professional gamers can make six figures plus, just like professional poker players."

With mention of the size of the market, Finley's mouth fell open in surprise.

Hunter snickered at her reaction. "I know! And, as you know, here at the Summit use of electronics is frowned upon. So we have this elaborate setup we use that hooks her phone up to this other box thing which connects to a monitor that we hide in the bottom of my suitcase. And then she's ready to play."

"And we need to get the hookup ready," Jillian said, giving Hunter's arm a gentle tug.

He reached over and shook Finley's hand before turning to give Charlie and Whitt long, heartfelt hugs.

"You really should consider coming back to play, even if for a short set," Charlie pleaded.

Hunter kidded good-naturedly, "Jilly would have my head. She doesn't like my music. Says it takes too much time—away from her."

Jillian had pulled him almost to the edge of the lobby pavilion when he turned and mouthed with a wink to Charlie, "But we'll see!"

The women returned to their seats in the lounge. Their tea had grown cold, so the staff had removed their cups and were brewing new pots of jasmine, matcha, and ginger tea. The sweet smell permeated the space.

"Well, that was interesting," Whitt mused as her ginger tea arrived. "I wouldn't have recognized him. In fact, I didn't."

"What's different now with him?" Finley asked before turning to Charlie. "And have you changed that much? He seemed to have remembered Whitt before he recognized you."

Charlie laughed. "A few highlights here and there have made my strawberry a bit blonder!"

Whitt was pensive. "As for me, I don't know that he has changed that much except for the beard. He didn't have one when we were together. I guess I haven't seen him in four-plus years, and I wasn't expecting him. I thought he was still in the UK. It took a while for my brain to process it all."

"Did you part on good terms, or was there drama?" Finley got straight to the point. She really wanted to know, to understand. Had something happened, or did they just drift apart and move on?

Charlie chortled at the question. "There certainly was drama. Well, at least for him. Whitt was over it, but Hunter wouldn't let go. He called her for almost a good six months after they broke up. Almost until he headed back to the UK. Whitt couldn't even come to our gigs."

"Whitt, you broke the man's heart? He couldn't bear being on the same continent without you, so he left?" Finley teased. "And you are so coldhearted that now you didn't even recognize him? Whoa, that's harsh."

"Oh, quit, you two!" Whitt play punched her sister. "Let's get to the real question: What's with his girlfriend? I know it can be boring to hear people you don't know catching up on history you don't care about, but even if you can't join in, let your boyfriend have his fun."

"And then not letting him play? He's a really good bassist!" Charlie was animated now. She couldn't imagine a life without music. "Not sure I'd let someone control me like that."

Finley sipped at her tea. "That's not the question I had. The real one for me is whether this is the Jillian that Melinda was talking about. She didn't seem klutzy to me."

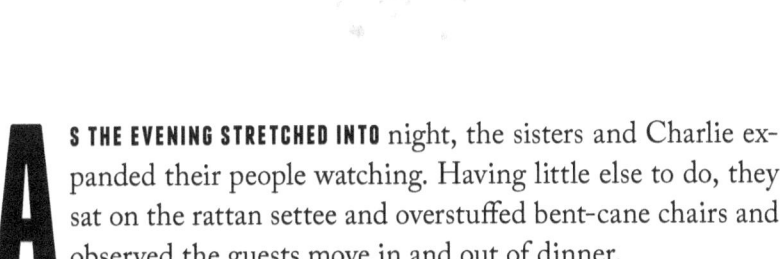

A **S THE EVENING STRETCHED INTO** night, the sisters and Charlie expanded their people watching. Having little else to do, they sat on the rattan settee and overstuffed bent-cane chairs and observed the guests move in and out of dinner.

The angle of the lobby lounge gave them a panoramic view of the resort's common areas as well as the divergent paths leading to the spa, pools, and villas. The communal pavilion that hosted morning meditation and yoga classes sat to the right of the lobby, with the dining room a bit behind it and to the left of the open-air structure. The lobby, dining area, and pavilion made a perfect triangle, which was the hub of activity most days. Tonight was no exception.

The threesome had finished two cups of tea and were perusing the menu for other options.

"What I wouldn't do for a glass of wine about now," Finley said under her breath.

"Or a glass of Pol Roger, with its perfectly structured inner spiral of tiny bubbles." Whitt waxed lyrical thinking of one of her favorite champagnes.

"I thought you two would be craving bourbon!" Charlie joked. She had seen the sisters in full southern-girl mode, enjoying fingers of their daddy's favorite distilled elixir.

"That might be too much to ask!" Finley smiled as she thought of the Van Winkle, Taylor, and Old Forester bottles her daddy had brought out for samplings during Whitt's wedding week. The poor bride had needed it with bodies and bones threatening her nuptials.

When the waiter brought their carob teas and pistachio matcha mousse, they had just completed a running commentary on the array of attire guests were wearing that evening.

Most of the men had settled on some sort of khaki pant and a cotton tee or untucked shirt as their evening uniform. The women, however, had dressed to match their personalities. Everything from voluminous patterned yoga pants to haute couture sundresses in tiny floral print were on display. The former had been sported by Lilith, while Angela and her sister wore the latter.

"I can't believe that Miss International is still there. It's been what, two hours plus?" Finley's eyes were glued on the center table where the beauty queen sat. The nannies and the children had long since left, with one bodyguard following them and the other keeping watch over Angela, her parents, and her sister.

"Where's the hubby, do you think?" Whitt asked, looking around the room in search of Angela's husband.

"He's over with Danny," Charlie remarked, glancing at two men who were standing near the dessert station, deep in conversation.

Finley eyed the two men. "When Danny came in for tea, Angela's husband jumped up and followed him. Do you think he is in the market for a yacht?"

"Do they have that much money?" Whitt wondered out loud. "I know the father does, but I don't think the parents like Angela's husband much. And he would need their help to buy it."

A sly smile crept up Charlie's lips as she tried to read the scene.

"It looks like hubby is trying to make more of a sale than Danny is, and I don't think Danny is buying it." The women looked over as

Danny stood sipping his tea with a noncommittal expression that bordered on bored.

Not the best way to make friends and sell to people. Has he already decided that the Pinedas can't afford what he's selling? Finley wondered.

"Very interesting dynamic," Whitt mused.

"What makes you say hubby and papa don't like each other?" Finley looked over at Angela's father sitting with the rest of the entourage before diverting her attention to her husband and Danny, the sales guy.

"Oh, there've been articles in the magazines that suggest there is some tension there, but who knows. You can never trust the tabloids." Whitt was also looking at Danny and Angela's husband. "I wonder which will turn out to be the better used car salesman? This is almost as interesting as Lilith dissing Ben."

"And who says we can't find something interesting to do when there are no phones, no TV, and no computers," Finley laughed. "The Blake sisters just turn into catty biotches!"

"That is not good for our characters! We were trying so hard to reform," Whitt added. "What would Mama say?"

Finley gave her sister a sarcastic glare and adopted her mama's soft southern accent. "Why bother? You know you're going to fall off the catty wagon before the end of the evening. Refine your skills rather than trying to reform them."

All three burst into peals of laughter that had Whitt wiping tears after a couple of minutes. When she looked up, she caught a glimpse of Melinda and Arun under the shelter of the communal pavilion.

They were deep into a conversation, if not a heated argument. Melinda was gesticulating, while Arun maintained a stoic countenance. Periodically, Melinda would shake her head in apparent disbelief before starting again with the wild hand motions. At times, Arun would step back or reposition himself on the pavilion, only to be followed by Melinda. In the final moments of the discussion, Melinda appeared to walk away before returning to Arun with her eyes wide. She pointed at him and poked his chest with her finger to emphasize her words.

"What's going on there?" Charlie whispered. "I never would have guessed Melinda could get that angry. Wish I was a fly on the wall."

"Or could read lips." Whitt was riveted on the two, who had now parted, with Arun standing under the pavilion shelter and Melinda stomping off down the path that led to the villas.

Arun remained in the empty space for several minutes before they saw him walk toward the bell hut at the front of the property. Some minutes later a red Porsche Cayman pulled up. The attendant handed Arun the keys. He promptly got in and drove down the palm-lined lane leading to the main road.

"Must admit I didn't see that coming," Whitt muttered. "What do you think they were arguing about? Had to be something big for him to drive off like that."

"Hard to say. Was *he* dallying with someone here?" Finley was alluding to Lilith and Ben. She could have understood if it were Jamie arguing with Lilith, but he seemed blissfully unaware of what his wife was doing. "This is becoming a little too *Desperate Housewives* for me."

"Then just drink your tea while I observe the dynamics. This is actually a study in human interactions. I am sure a sociologist would be eating this up." Whitt scanned the room looking for another encounter to analyze.

"Yes, but you are not a sociologist, sister of mine." Finley smirked. "You're just a gossip. A good one, but still a gossip."

Whitt feigned insult while Charlie snickered. "You two are an attraction in itself! I'm having fun watching you watch everybody else." Charlie covered her mouth to stifle her laughter.

"Am I imagining things or did Angela's sister just slip off with the assistant?" Whitt's head remained fixed while her eyes cut sharply to the right.

Finley was able to catch sight of two clasped hands and the tail end of a flowy patterned dress before the image rounded the edge of the building and was gone.

"Sorry, kid. All I saw was the skirt of a dress. I couldn't tell you the color, style—or who was in it," Finley kidded. "You are too fast for me."

Charlie suddenly sat up in her chair, craning her neck and lasering her eyes on the figure that moved quietly through the dark to the entry driveway pulling an overnight bag. "Is that Noelle?"

Finley and Whitt both trained their eyes on the shadowy outline that moved through the darkness. All three were up and moving toward the image before any of them answered.

"Noelle?" Finley called out softly.

The figure stopped and turned in the dark toward the women. "Yes?" The women could see the person trying to discern who was speaking from the shadows.

"It's Finley, Whitt, and Charlie. Are you leaving?" Finley was almost up on the woman by now.

The figure stopped just short of the entryway light. Finley moved to stand fully in the light so she could see the woman's face.

"Yes." Noelle fidgeted with the identification tag on the strap of her suitcase. "This morning was just too unsettling. I'll come back another time. Maybe."

Finley reached out and touched her arm. "I'm so sorry that your stay was disrupted. Hope your trip back is smooth. Travel safely."

Noelle accepted the well wishes and turned to give Finley and the other women a hug. She moved forward as the car taking her to the airport pulled into the circle. She sighed sadly. "I suspect you have more to worry about than I do. Do look after yourselves."

The threesome watched as she passed her suitcase to the driver and settled herself in the back seat. She waved as the car pulled off and down the drive.

"That's two gone. And the wrong two! Why can't Miss International or the Sanderford posse exit the premises?" Whitt asked as they caught the light of the car as it faded onto the main road.

"Not sure there will be any more drama tonight," Finley observed. "What say we just head back to the rooms and chill out there."

Charlie nodded. "Sounds good to me. We have early massages tomorrow, so we probably should turn in early."

Finley gave no indication of agreement other than to start down the path leading to the rooms. After only a few steps, she paused and watched as Ben and a woman, half hidden by the shadows, continued along the parallel path that ran on the other side of the community pavilion. He and the woman walked arm in arm, laughing jovially as they went. Finley assumed he had made up with Lilith since the Great Snub. She stifled a gasp when the woman's face came into the light and she saw that Melinda, not Lilith, was Ben's companion.

The twosome was so engrossed in conversation that they seemed oblivious to anyone or anything around them. There were only a few other guests on the paths, and most were heading to their rooms. At the junction, Ben and Melinda followed the path toward the now deserted therapy rooms and were soon lost to the darkness.

"Well, I bet we know where they're going!" Finley quipped as they all stood planted on the path. "I'm not sure what just happened, but I have a good idea of what's going to happen next."

"I'm confused." Charlie bit on her lip and stared down the path behind the shadow of Ben and Melinda. "This morning all was right with the world between Melinda and Arun. Then something happened and they argued and now only an hour or so later, she's moved on to someone else?"

Whitt nodded confirmation to her friend. "That pretty much sums it up. Who knew? Melinda would have been the last person I would have pegged as flighty. And yet . . ."

"We don't know. Maybe she had given Arun an ultimatum and he blew it off. So she said toodles and moved on," Finley speculated.

"Even so, that's a pretty quick rebound. I mean, she could have waited until tomorrow at least. What if he comes back?" Whitt turned quickly toward the drive. "That would be an unholy mess."

"You can say that again." Finley chuckled at the prospect of Arun finding Melinda and Ben together.

"Well, it's not our battle. You guys up for a round of Texas Hold'em?" Charlie asked as they rounded the corner to their villa.

Once in the room and settled in their nighties with yet another cup of tea, the threesome turned to a rambunctious round of cards. Charlie proved the master of the poker face, winning all but one of the seven hands played.

"How do you do that?" Whitt exclaimed. She stared at her friend, who sat smugly raking in the pile of coins that had been deposited on the table.

"Practice!" was all Charlie said with a smirk. "Practice!"

"Do you have brothers, Charlie?" Finley asked.

"Two, and one sister. And they all are competitive," Charlie replied. "I'm the youngest. Winning was the only way to get respect."

Finley nodded in understanding. She wondered whether Whitt had ever felt the need to beat her to win her respect. The six-year age difference may have mitigated the need.

But maybe she just never said anything and was trying to best me all along, Finley considered.

"So what's the deal with Melinda?" Whitt blurted out mid-deal at the start of the eighth game. "The argument was a surprise, but the rebound was even more startling."

"Guess she just got fed up and decided there were other fish in the sea." Finley put down her cards, evidence of her first win of the night.

"What? I almost had a winning hand!" Whitt cried as Finley's cards hit the table.

"And too bad about Noelle." Charlie gathered the played cards, stacked them with the others, and began to shuffle. "Who would do such a thing? And why?"

"That's the thing. Do you think it was just a joke or specifically planned for her?" Finley looked at the hand Charlie had just dealt her and frowned.

Whitt grinned at her sister's reaction to her cards. "Hard to say. We don't know enough about any of these people to figure out if there's any connection beyond what we can readily see."

"You've got a point," Charlie said. "We know that each of the couples know each other. Melinda and Noelle knew each other from other trips to the Summit, and Melinda knew Jillian from school. We know Hunter."

"Some better than others," Finley interjected before being silenced by a jab from her sister.

Charlie giggled at the sisters' jousting and continued, "And Arun knew Mark or some member of his team since he is considering a yacht."

Finley threw down a card and thought about what Charlie said. "I'm not sure where that gets us if we can't figure out the thread that connects them all."

The three went quiet, pondering their cards and trying to ferret out the possible links between the guests at the Summit.

"What was that?" Finley asked as she quickly placed her cards face down on the table and got up. "Did you hear that?"

Finley opened the door to the patio and walked toward the railing of the large deck that housed the pool. Hanging over the jungle ravine below, during the day, it looked like the mouth of a waterfall. At night, however, it loomed large, like the gullet of a beast.

Finley stood, turning her ear toward the jungle. All was still as she waited. Nothing but the screech of the macaques in the trees.

"What did you hear?" Whitt asked as she and Charlie joined her sister on the overhang.

"Sounded like a cry, but it was just for a second," Finley relayed, her head still inclined toward the jungle. "Strange. Probably just a monkey in heat."

Charlie and Whitt laughed as they headed back inside. "She's projecting," Whitt declared, shaking her head. "Poor girl's missing Max so much, she's hearing things."

"ARE YOU ASLEEP?" WHITT STOOD over her sister the next morning, peering down at her prone figure.

"I was, but I guess I'm not now. What time is it?"

"Just after eight. We have massages at eleven."

"Then I guess we'd better get dressed, but I don't want to," Finley moaned, her eyes clenched shut. "Is Charlie up?"

Charlie stood at the door to Finley's room, stretching. "Yep. That was a good sleep."

"If I wasn't sure that this was a 'dry' spa, I would have sworn they put something in the tea." Finley yawned and pulled the covers back over her head.

"Up with you, lazy bones!" Whitt played tug-of-war with Finley over the blanket, finally snatching it back, leaving Finley with just the sheet.

"All right, already. I'm up." Finley swung her legs off the bed and sprang to her feet.

"I can't believe you. Normally, I am the lugabed." Whitt chuckled at Finley's closed-eye stumble toward the bathroom.

"That's what I'm saying! They put something in my tea!"

"I doubt that. You're just having severe coffee withdrawal."

"They might have some black tea stashed somewhere, if we ask nicely," Charlie offered.

"I doubt it. The caffeine police have already sniffed it out and confiscated whatever reserves have been put aside. A few more days. Only a few more days," Finley muttered as she stepped into the shower.

Less than an hour later, the threesome was dressed and ready for some food. The dining room was far less crowded than it had been the night before.

"Probably sleeping it off, like we did," Finley remarked as she scanned the menu for something that she hadn't had before.

"Speak for yourself. Neither Charlie nor I had any problem getting up. You're just getting old!" Whitt joked.

Charlie shook her head as Whitt skillfully dodged her sister's jab in the ribs before being caught with a playful kick in the shin.

"Oww!" Whitt mimed.

"Stop whining. I barely touched you," Finley countered. "Decide what you want. I'm hungry."

"Grouchy, aren't we! You've decided already?" Whitt looked up from the menu in surprise before returning to peruse the options.

"We should know it by heart by now, I suppose." Charlie picked up her teacup and glanced around the room. She noticed Melinda sitting alone at one of the patio tables.

Whitt closed her menu and followed Charlie's line of sight. Melinda had pulled on dark glasses and a sun hat even though the sun was masked by the clouds. She occupied herself with what appeared to be a crossword puzzle. Arun was nowhere to be seen. And neither was Ben.

Before Whitt could share her observation, Ben entered the dining room, weaving slowly between the tables, his eyes searching the seated guests as he went. Spying Melinda outside, he picked up his pace. When he reached her table, Melinda looked up and moved her satchel without speaking. The two sat side by side, reviewing the menu without a word. Even after the waiter came and took their order, the two were silent. After a time, Ben reached over and took Melinda's hand.

"Well, I'll be! Didn't take them long." Whitt raised an eyebrow and snickered.

"That's what you said last night." Finley looked around for the waiter who had taken Melinda and Ben's order, but he had slipped away before she could catch his eye.

"And the comment still stands. It didn't take her long," Whitt repeated. "They are such an odd couple, though."

"In what way?" Charlie asked, turning her attention to the couple, who still sat in silence. "They sort of match. He's a hippie and she's kind of a free spirit, I guess."

"I suppose. But after hanging with a rich Bollywood star, I wouldn't have thought she would have turned to a penniless yogi!" Whitt too was looking around for a waiter.

"Who says he's penniless? He might be a Richard Branson–like entrepreneur who contributes his spiritual services to needy patrons at spas like this." Finley could barely keep a straight face.

She doubted that Ben had more than two nickels to rub together beyond what he earned working at the Summit. If anyone looked the part of a wayward hipster, it was Ben.

"I wonder how Lilith is going to react to this latest development." Whitt caught a waiter's eye and signaled him over.

Orders in, the three women returned to the possible love triangle.

"Lilith snubbed him. I shouldn't think she would have much right to say anything. And she's married, besides," Charlie reminded them.

Whitt chortled. "Since when did that ever stop anyone? They better hope she doesn't see them. She looks like one of those soccer moms who would just snap and shoot the lot of them, leaving the hubby, kids, and other Stepford wives in the neighborhood puzzled. 'She was always the nicest of moms!'"

"That's cold! But now that you say it, there is a little iciness in her." Finley ran her eyes around the room to see if Lilith had walked in.

"Enough of them, what about us?" Whitt prepared to tuck into her vegan pancakes, a fluffy disk on which fresh mangoes, dragon fruit, and strawberries had been arrayed.

"What *about* us?" Finley asked, returning to her eggless shakshuka.

"What are we going to do today? I can't remember what I signed up for. It seems so long ago."

"It was only the day before yesterday. Now who's getting old?" Finley smirked.

Charlie intervened before Whitt and Finley had a rematch of their sisterly jousting. "As I recall, you and I are getting herbal wraps, and Finley is doing a reiki."

"Oh, now I remember. That will take us to lunch," Whitt said. "What are we going to do for the next couple of hours, until our treatments?"

"I, for one, am fine with lolling by the pool and taking it slow." Finley diverted her eyes in the direction of the pool.

"You can do that this afternoon. Let's try for a little exercise, at least," Whitt retorted. "Do you think your old bones can tolerate a leisurely walk around the grounds?"

Finley pushed back her chair and headed for the path. "You're on."

To the casual observer, the leisurely stroll turned into a power walk with each sister trying to outdo the other. After twenty minutes of racing each other, Finley finally plopped down on one of the benches.

"I give. You win. I'm tired." Finley wiped the sweat from her brow with a tissue she had stuffed in her pants pocket.

"I was wondering when you were going to slow down. I was fading fast," Whitt said with a sly grin. "Well, we got our exercise in."

"I am going to run back to the room to take a quick shower. I don't want that poor masseuse putting her hands on all this sweat."

"Now you've shamed me into doing the same. Charlie is the only one that used some common sense!" Whitt watched as Charlie ambled up to the sisters' bench, having slowly followed behind as the two raced up the path.

"I think I'll wait here for you." Charlie swapped places with the other two when they rose to head to the room.

"Hoping hunky Cam will saunter by?" Whitt teased.

Charlie's face reddened. "That never occurred to me. I guess it would look a bit odd, me just sitting there, doing nothing but waiting."

"Charlie, you take your rest. Whitt was just joking," Finley assured her.

Charlie pushed up from the bench and joined Finley and Whitt on the path. "Maybe . . . just the same, I think I can find something to do in the room while you guys clean up."

Finley didn't protest further, but she shot her sister a withering glance.

The threesome had rounded the side path that led to their villa when Finley caught something out of the corner of her eye. A flash in the underbrush that covered the ravine over which their balcony hung.

"Where are you going?" Whitt called to Finley, seeing her leave the path and walk to the edge of the retaining wall that ran along the lip of the cliff that headed the ravine.

"I thought I saw something down there . . ." Finley's voice trailed off as she scanned the landscape. "There!"

Whitt and Charlie hurried over to where Finley stood and directed their attention to the section of terrain where she was pointing.

"I don't see anything. Where are you looking?" Whitt crowded closer to Finley, squinting to follow her sister's sight line.

"There!" Charlie pointed to some underbrush midway down the hill. "It looks like a mirror or something flashing. Come over to this side. You might catch it better."

As Whitt moved slightly to her right, a short burst of light caught her eye. "What is that?"

"I don't know, but it might be connected to that sound I heard last night. Someone may have fallen and gotten hurt." Finley cut across the grass at a jog. She opened the door and headed straight for the phone.

"Reception? This is Finley Blake in the Pool Villa. I see something in the ravine and think it might be a guest who needs assistance."

Within seconds, Whitt was by her side trying to shush her. "You don't know that! It could just be a discarded bottle catching the sun. We're going to look awfully foolish."

"Better safe than sorry," Finley countered, her hand over the mouthpiece. "If you had slipped and fallen and were using a mirror or your glasses or your watch face to catch someone's attention and they ignored you, how would you feel? I'm willing to look silly on the outside chance that it is not a piece of trash but rather someone asking for help."

Whitt relented reluctantly and took a seat on the couch that looked out toward the ravine. She could still see the bright reflection of the sun off whatever was down there.

"Ms. Blake?" Several minutes later, Mr. Flores, the hotel manager, rapped on the doorframe. He hesitated a moment before sticking his head in the door. He stopped short of entering, standing on the threshold waiting for permission.

Finley stood to greet him. She took him by the elbow to turn him around and lead him back outside to the ravine.

"Yes, let me show you what we saw." Finley pointed in the direction from which the flash of light had come. It still shone as a periodic burst of white rays in the lush green underbrush. "There!"

Mr. Flores drew back and shaded his eyes from the glare that momentarily blinded him. "What is that?"

"That's what we hoped you would find out," Finley replied.

"It's probably trash that someone tossed," the manager suggested offhandedly.

Whitt decided to join in the fun. "Are you saying that the grounds are not surveyed for trash daily?"

Well, I'll be. She clearly has forgotten that she said the same thing the manager had less than twenty minutes ago. She must really dislike the man. Finley chuckled at the exchange between her sister and Mr. Flores.

The manager, clearly taken aback at the suggestion that his property was not well maintained, sputtered. "No, no, you misunderstood me. We do not have trash lying about. But we may have overlooked some minor objects. In any event, we will investigate. Rest assured."

With that, Mr. Flores turned and scurried down the path, barking out orders to staff as he went.

Finley, Whitt, and Charlie watched from their balcony as, within minutes of Mr. Flores's departure, three of the larger male staff members came to the lip of the ravine and stood looking down.

"They must be trying to figure out how to get down to that area. Aren't there paths that cross that way?" Whitt peered over the balcony edge, looking for the footpaths, but the foliage blocked a clear view.

"I don't think there are paths on this side of the hill. It's just jungle," Charlie observed.

"Everything all right, ladies?" The women turned quickly to see Cam standing on the villa sidewalk, trying to see what they were looking at. "I was coming from a tennis lesson with Sanderford. What's going on?"

"We saw something in the bush in the ravine, and the hotel is trying to figure out what it is," Whitt shared.

Finley smiled at Whitt's strategic use of the royal "we."

Cam moved closer to the balcony railing—and Charlie. "Do they think it's a guest?"

"I don't think anyone knows. It looks like they have called in specialized equipment," Charlie responded, taking a quick glance at Cam.

"Seems so. This looks pretty serious. I guess I should go and see what help I can lend. See you ladies later." Cam smiled at Charlie before heading toward reception.

After giving Charlie a round of ribbing, the women turned their attention back to the activities at the edge of the ravine. Men in some sort of official garb had joined the other staff members at the retaining wall at the top of the ravine. Mr. Flores was gesturing, pointing between the women's villa and the spot on the hillside. Hotel guests had now left their spa activities and gathered on the lawn overlooking the ravine. Finley could make out the figures of Melinda, Ben, Anya, and the Anderson family among them.

"We'd better hop in the shower if we are going to make our massages," Finley said suddenly, leaving her position on the balcony to head into the villa.

When she returned from her shower some minutes later, she could see from her balcony that the men in military-like uniforms were pulling something—or someone—up the steep incline in a sheet-wrapped gurney.

"That doesn't look good," Finley said, pulling her robe tighter as if to ward off the bad energy the scene was giving off. Whitt and Charlie had moved from the grass to the balcony and were seated watching the action.

"Looks like they found something. And whatever it was, they put it on the gurney and brought it up," Whitt relayed.

"Is it a body?"

"Hard to say."

"But you don't generally wrap anything other than a body in a sheet," Charlie observed.

Finley looked across to the group gathered near reception. She could see even from that distance that the hotel manager had blanched, stumbling backward at the sight of the gurney or at something the retrieval team had told him. He moved, trancelike, among the gathered staff, giving instructions but almost in slow motion.

"I guess we'd better check to see if our massages are still on," Finley proposed as she headed back into the villa. Whitt and Charlie followed her in.

While Whitt cleaned up, Finley and Charlie reviewed the events of the past couple of days.

"Something weird is going on here." Finley had poured herself and Charlie a cup of tea as they sat waiting for Whitt.

"You're telling me. Two deaths in two days. And you know Mr. Flores is going to want to hush this up, too."

"They have to be connected." Finley paused and stared at Charlie. "Do you think they have to do with Sanderford?"

"If he is involved, I feel for Anya and the other ladies."

Some minutes later, the three women headed to the spa pavilion. Strangely enough, none of the sessions had been canceled, but the times had been pushed back to accommodate the guests who had interrupted their massages to see what all the fuss was about.

The women decided to sit by the pool until they were called. After ordering a round of mango matcha smoothies, they sat eavesdropping on some of the other guests talking about what had happened that morning.

"Well, I heard that Mr. Flores, such a lovely man, got a tip-off that there was a body down there. The tipster was probably in cahoots with the killer." A middle-aged Australian woman, with a high-pitched voice that had Whitt trying to discreetly cover her ears when she spoke, was giving a rundown to her seatmates of what had occurred.

"Did anyone find out who it was?" asked a man with a nascent beer belly seated with his wife, a shapely woman several years younger than him.

"Cyril, they haven't caught the killer yet," the Australian woman replied. She and the man looked like they could be related. Possibly siblings.

"Not the killer, Astrid! The body. Who was it in the ravine?" Cyril snapped.

His wife stood, adjusting her bathing cap as she headed for the pool. "But who's to say it wasn't an accident? Everyone just jumps to murder. The person could have just slipped and fallen."

Her husband waited until she dove into the pool before responding. "So naive! So trusting! You don't just slip over a retaining wall that high. Someone had to help you over."

At that, Finley, Whitt, and Charlie were called into their massages. When they returned to the pool area afterward, the Australian woman and the couple were gone.

Finley signaled for a waiter. "Three waters, or do you want something else?"

"Water is fine for now," Charlie replied, and Whitt nodded her assent.

"As relaxing as that was, I couldn't help but turn over in my mind what those people were talking about while we were waiting for our treatments." Whitt had stretched out on one of the lounge chairs and closed her eyes, still in a post-massage Zen.

"Yeah, was it an accident or murder? And who was it who died?" Finley stood over her until she decided to join her on another chaise.

"Maybe I can help with some of those answers," a deep baritone offered.

Finley looked up to see Evans standing nearby and Cam approaching. "Evans, I haven't seen you around. Are you involved in these goings-on?"

Cam caught Charlie's eye and winked, almost causing Charlie to miss the edge of her seat when she sat down. She returned his wink with a smile.

In the meantime, Whitt had roused herself from her stupor and was all attention. "Please fill us in. We only caught the beginning of the saga."

"Cam said you were the ones that called reception. What did you see?" Evans had seated himself at the foot of Finley's lounge chair while Cam pulled up a plastic chair and sat beside Charlie.

"Finley saw it first. A flash of light in the underbrush. She kept insisting that maybe one of the guests was in trouble," Whitt explained. "So she called reception, and they sent Mr. Flores out."

"Flores himself came out?" Cam seemed surprised.

"I guess he figured if it was another body, he wanted to manage Finley himself." Whitt laughed, referring to the exchange between Finley and the hotel manager when they had found the first body at the falls.

"So, who was it? A guest?" Finley inquired.

"Of sorts. It was one of the Pineda party's bodyguards. They had reported him missing this morning," Evans stated.

"Actually, it was one of the other members of her staff who said he hadn't returned to his room last night. Mrs. Pineda herself had little interest in finding him. Kept passing the security guys' questions off to one of her other guards. When they told her they found him dead, she just threw up her hand and flounced away," Cam added.

Whitt shook her head. "That's sad. You would think you would care about the people that look after you and your family."

"Lives of the rich and famous," Finley muttered under her breath.

"What did they say happened?" Charlie directed her question at Cam.

Cam turned to fully engage her. "Broken neck."

"From the fall or before?" Finley squinted in concentration.

"We think it was before, but we couldn't get that close to the body to check," Evans answered, his eyes on Finley as he spoke.

"So, we are talking murder, then?" Finley swallowed hard.

Evans nodded. "Second one in two days."

"That's what Charlie said. Do you think they are connected? More importantly, are they connected to you know who?" Finley anticipated the answer. "What's your next step?"

Evans snickered under his breath. "I should have known you guys would figure it out."

"We've only identified the problem. We don't have an answer." Finley bit her lip and creased her brow.

"Nope, but I know you will in time. But please don't do anything—and I mean anything—without letting me or Cam know. This is too dangerous." Evans got to his feet. He smiled at Finley before looking over at Whitt, who had been strangely quiet during the conversation. "I mean it!"

The sisters had heard warnings from Evans almost every time they encountered him. Try as they might, they hadn't been able to heed his admonition yet. *Bodies find us. We don't go looking for them!* Finley had once said.

As he was leaving, Cam sidled up to Charlie. "You up for a run this afternoon? I had a cancellation and thought you might be interested in the slot."

Charlie paused for a moment before nodding.

"Good. See you at one thirty at the yoga pavilion," Cam replied before striking off behind Evans.

"I bet you will!" Whitt playfully tapped Charlie's shoulder. "We'd better get you some fuel before you and Cam run off together!"

9

CAM PICKED CHARLIE UP FOR their run right after lunch. Charlie had had just enough time to return to the villa and change into her running gear before taking off for the pavilion. She arrived just as Cam was walking up.

"Slow down. You're not late. And even if you were, I wasn't going to leave you." Cam ambled over to Charlie and took her hand.

Charlie started to pull back until she realized that Cam only wanted to check her heart rate.

"Nice steady rhythm there." Cam dropped her arm and turned toward the paths that ran behind the villas.

Charlie began to breathe more slowly. "What was my heart rate?"

"Seventy-eight. Is it in line with your normal?"

"A little faster." Charlie had to acknowledge that the reason for the faster heart rate was standing in front of her.

Cam grinned before considering the paths again. "Any preference for the route we take?"

"No. I'll leave it to you."

"How long a run are you up for? Hills? No hills? These paths have it all."

"No hills, that much I know. And I don't have any treatments scheduled for today."

"Okay, let's take it slow and add some challenge as we go. If you get tired, you know how to say slow it down or stop. You aren't going to hurt my feelings. This is my second run today, so I may tap out before you do."

"Your second? How long was the first?" Charlie was now curious about whether the trainer cover was really reflective of the man behind it.

"Yep. Had one with Sanderford this morning. It was pretty short though. He was an hour late and then started complaining about the heat, as if I have a temperature regulator to change the weather at will. Enough about that. Let's get started."

Cam had started the run before Charlie even knew she was running. She'd had to racewalk to keep up with his long legs and had transitioned into a jog easily. Cam kept a nice, even pace that matched her natural running rhythm.

"So, how are you liking Manila?" Cam asked as they reached the two-kilometer mark on the upper trail that skirted the jungle and followed the upper ridge with a view of the ocean.

"Manila's okay, but it's places like this, outside the city, that are the real Philippines." She looked over at the water as they ran. That high above the shoreline almost above the first tree canopy, she could see miles and miles of cerulean, aquamarine, and indigo.

"We have a few more kilometers to go before you see the real view."

"I should ask you what you think about the country. I've lived here for years, but you've only been here for a short while."

"Yes. Just over a year. When I left the navy, I started doing some contracting work around Asia and ended up back here. Got introduced to Evans and this assignment."

"Had you met Evans before?"

"Actually, no. Seems like a good guy. You guys seem to know him pretty well."

"Finley and Whitt do. I just met him in Charleston, at Whitt's wedding."

"How long have they been married?"

"About six months."

"And Finley?"

"She and Max have been together like forever but only formally partnered for a couple of years. Max doesn't believe in marriage, I don't think."

"And you?"

"And me what? I'm not married."

"Partnered?"

"No." Charlie chuckled at the line of questioning.

"Believe in marriage?"

"What?"

"Do you believe in marriage?"

"Don't know that there's anything to believe in. It's a good institution. With the right person. But only with the right person."

"And I take it you haven't found the right person?"

"No. Not yet."

"Hmm." Cam cast a side glance at Charlie, who was shaking her head and smiling. "Only another two klicks and we're there."

"And then we have to run back!"

"We set a pretty fast pace going up—we'll have done ten kilometers in about an hour. So we can slow it down going back."

Charlie took in air and sighed but never broke pace until she and Cam reached the lookout point. There she paused, her hands on her hips, and took in the view. The strands of blue she had seen earlier as one-sided now wrapped around her on three sides.

"This is spectacular. It never ceases to amaze me how each island in the Philippines can have such different hues of water. And all of it beautiful." Charlie could see slivers of golden sand in certain parts of the panorama, but for much of it, it felt as if she were suspended over the water.

For several minutes the two of them were silently perched on a boulder, listening to the wind in the palms, watching the waves rise and crash, feeling the breeze cool the sweat on their faces and bodies.

Cam broke the silence. "You ready to head back or you want to stay for a bit longer?"

"We can start back. I don't want to cool down too much. I may not be able to move if I do," Charlie kidded.

"Okay, then. Let's go."

As they came back onto the resort grounds some fifty minutes later, they saw the Anderson clan settling themselves by the pool. While Jamie took a dip, the kids stretched out on the lounge chairs, their heads bent low over their Switches. Lilith checked her phone before gathering up her towel and satchel and waving goodbye to her husband and children, who failed to return her farewell.

"You up for a swim after we clean up?" Cam asked as he and Charlie walked to the locker room.

"Sure. Salt pool or regular?"

"Let's do salt pool. A little less crowded."

They had almost reached the split for the locker rooms when they saw Lilith outside the yoga studio peering in. She alternated between checking the time on her watch and rattling the door to the studio. After the third or fourth time, Lilith kicked a nearby trash can and cursed under her breath.

She turned quickly without looking up and almost ran into Charlie and Cam.

"I thought I had a session today. I guess not," she mumbled as she walked away. "Damn!" was the last thing they heard.

Cam glanced at Charlie, raised an eyebrow, and shrugged. "See you in the salt pool."

As she showered and pulled on her swimsuit, Charlie considered how different her encounters with Lilith at the yoga studio had been. In the course of little over a day, Lilith had gone from paramour to betrayed, and she wasn't taking it well.

"That was an unusual scene outside the studio," Cam observed when they both were in the salt pool.

"That's an understatement." Charlie decided against telling him about the earlier encounter in which Ben had a hand. That was for Lilith to tell, if ever she would.

While she talked, Charlie cast an appreciative glance over Cam's fit form. She had noticed him doing the same to her when she threw off her cover-up to get into the pool, so she thought it only fair that she assess his packaging as well. Tanned from all the time on the paths and tennis court and broad-shouldered with an enviable six-pack, he was what the sisters' cousin Odessa would say was a "fine-looking man."

She decided to change the subject to something less distracting. "What's this salt water supposed to do?"

"It's supposed to support the immune system by detoxifying and calming it. Salt particles are reputed to help your breathing, too."

Charlie pursed her lips and wrinkled her face with each claim Cam made in support of saltwater pools.

"You don't seem convinced." Cam gave her a crooked smile. "Don't shoot the messenger. That's what they say."

"Well, it doesn't hurt my eyes as much as chlorine does. So, I'll give it one point, but the rest I'll wait to see."

"A natural skeptic." He was bobbing up and down in the pool, a difficult feat given the buoyancy of the water. "What else don't you believe? That Santa is real? That the tooth fairy really has a wall with teeth on it, including yours? That the Easter Bunny poops chocolate eggs?"

Charlie almost snorted in water at the last comment. "Whoever told you that one about the Easter Bunny?"

"So, you do believe the others. It's just the Easter Bunny that you doubt?"

"No. Well, yes. But no. You have me confused." Charlie splashed water in mock frustration. "I don't believe in any of them—although the Blake sisters still believe in all of them. I don't know if they have ever been told about the bunny and the eggs, though."

"You can't be serious. Santa?"

"Yep. Finley told me that I was a Doubting Charlie. That if it wasn't Santa who brought them, then how did I explain those presents under the tree that I had wished for and somehow magically gotten."

"What did you say?"

"Nothing. I could have attributed it to Whitt or Mama or Max or Daddy eavesdropping, but the wonder and trust in her eyes kept me quiet. She believes, and that's all that matters. It almost made me jealous." Charlie smiled and cast off the thought with a gentle shrug. "What about you? What do you believe in?"

"I guess I'm a lot like your friends. I've been blessed in so many ways by things I can't understand."

"Like what?"

"Life. If you look close, you'll see little scars on my chest and back. Shrapnel. From my last deployment. I wasn't supposed to live. But I did."

Charlie had noticed the slight raised marks on his otherwise smooth chest but hadn't paid much attention to them. Now she looked more closely.

"I'm glad you did, too," she whispered under her breath.

When Charlie got back to the villa, Finley and Whitt were out back near the villa's private dunk pool. Barely larger than a king-size bed, the pool was perfect for cooling off and the patio was a good space for relaxing. And that was what the sisters were doing—relaxing. While Whitt read through what appeared to be economic reports, Finley was scrolling through the frames of pictures she had shot with Max earlier in the week.

"Well, how was it?" Whitt looked up from her work as soon as Charlie walked through the door.

"Nice," Charlie said, her smile saying the rest.

"And?" Whitt leaned forward in the chaise as if that movement might squeeze a bit more information out of Charlie.

"Whitt, leave her alone. You of all people should understand the need to process emotions."

"Me? If I feel it, I say it. Well, at least now I do after being with David. It's you that wallows in your feelings."

Finley chuckled. "That's true. I was just trying to imbue you with a more complex range of emotions. Sorry."

Whitt threw her pencil at her sister. It fell short and wide, landing at Charlie's feet instead.

"Charlie, did you have a good run? Which path did you take?" While Finley wasn't a runner, she had covered most of the paths on her picture-taking outings over the last few days.

"The upper ridge. I hadn't ever taken that path. It was spectacular. The water had so many bands of color." Charlie picked up the pencil and handed it to Whitt.

"I've walked it for a short distance, but Dalisay said there was a lookout a few miles down the path."

"That's where we ran. To the lookout and back."

"Is that far?" Whitt asked.

"About ten kilometers. It only took about an hour. It was a nice run."

Whitt was relentless. "Well, if it only took an hour there and an hour back, what have you been doing for the last hour?"

"Swimming." Charlie wasn't sure whether to mention her encounter with Lilith.

"And?" Whitt asked again.

"And nothing. We talked. As I said, he's really nice."

"And?"

"And he's easy to talk to."

"And?"

"He makes me laugh. And what else do you want to know?" Charlie laughed at Whitt's inquisition.

"Good gracious, Whitt. I don't think you ever questioned me about Max like that. I'm not sure I could have stood the pressure." Finley thought about their time in Morocco together, the second time she and Max were together.

"I wouldn't have dared. You were too fragile. Charlie's made of sterner stuff and asked me the same questions early on with David," Whitt said.

Finley realized Whitt had made the comment in jest, but there was a lot of truth in what her sister said. She had been so fragile after her breakup with Max, and even when they reconnected during the second trip to Morocco. Even now, there were some parts of their relationship that she wasn't sure she could explain to anyone but Max. Their difficult history was their bond.

"Well, Charlie, I'm glad you had an enjoyable afternoon," Finley remarked. "We were waiting for you before we headed to the lounge for a predinner mocktail."

"That sounds lovely. Let me change out of these shorts into a longer pair of pants. The mosquitoes will have a field day on my legs, if not."

The lobby bar was rather deserted. There were a few couples sitting out on the patio finishing tea before they went to dress for dinner. Finley, Whitt, and Charlie had decided to dress for dinner before they went to the lounge so they could go to the dining room without having to change again.

"What are you guys going for tonight? Tea or a mocktail?" Charlie asked as she looked at the drinks menu.

"I think I am going for the 'drink of the night'—a hibiscus highball," Finley announced.

"That sounds good. I'll make that two."

"Three," Whitt chimed in.

The waiter had just served their order when Whitt interrupted their conversation.

"Hey, isn't that Arun?" She directed the others' attention to the far side of the yoga pavilion. A man of Arun's height and build was walking toward the villas.

"I thought he had left. If Melinda is with Ben, it could be awkward." Finley watched as Arun was lost behind a large palm.

"Well, it's going to be awkward, then, because Melinda was with Ben," Charlie shared. "Cam and I saw them heading to the sauna together as we were leaving the pool."

"Oh dear. That's not going to play out well." Finley wondered at what point in the evening the Melinda/Ben/Arun drama would begin. If the gods were with them, it was possible that Arun might never run into them on a property this large, but then again, the setting seemed more fitting for a full-scale spectacle.

"And Lilith might add some fuel to the fire."

"What do you mean?" Whitt asked.

"Seems Ben blew her off this afternoon. She was hanging out near the yoga studio. Then Cam and I saw her skulking around when Melinda and Ben went to the sauna. She didn't look happy."

"Damn!" Whitt whistled. "This is getting complicated."

"You can say that again. A play in four parts—Melinda and Arun, Ben and Lilith, Melinda and Ben, and then Ben and Arun." Finley shook her head at the magnitude of a scene there might be if this all came to a head in a public space like the pavilion or the studio.

Charlie frowned. "Not to mention Lilith's husband."

"Apparently, the play has a few more parts." Whitt gave a dastardly chuckle. "Now we have to add Ben and Jamie *and* Melinda and Lilith. The plot thickens."

"Goodness, I had completely forgotten Jamie. Invisible creatures can become quite violent when they decide to be noticed." Finley was trying to contemplate Jamie's possible reaction when he found out his wife was cheating on him. Tuck his tail and go home? Or come out, guns blazing? It was anybody's guess. He was too invisible to tell.

The threesome was walking back from dinner, along the path that ran between the pool and the spa area. The compound was practically deserted, populated by only a few late diners who, like the women, were enjoying the moonlit night. The rest of the guests were in their rooms, many already asleep. The sisters and Charlie had lingered over their drinks in the lounge, so they were some of the last to be served in the dining room.

They had just reached the green when a piercing scream rent the quiet night. All three turned in different directions, searching for the source of the sound that was now echoing off buildings in the recreational compound.

"Where did that come from?" Finley stood in place, listening hard for other activity that might help orient her to the location of the screamer.

"I think it was in the spa center." Whitt had already started backtracking. The others were close on her heels.

A small group had gathered at the door of the sauna. One of the guests was comforting Marisol, one of the spa attendants, who was hysterical. Her *pinya* blouse was wet with tears, and her shoulders racked with sobs.

Finley approached a man, presumably the husband of the woman ministering to Marisol. "What happened?"

"An accident. A guest has been injured, likely fatally. Reception and the snake handler have been called."

"Snake handler? Why? Is there a viper in there?" Whitt stepped back. "If so, why don't they close the door before it escapes?"

The man stepped aside to give the threesome a better view of the scene. There, on the sauna bench, wrapped in a large black python's coil, was Melinda.

"Is she dead?" Charlie whispered.

Finley nodded. The multiact drama was not playing out as she had imagined. The ending was far more deadly.

10

"**WHAT IN BLAZES IS GOING** on?" Evans had knocked on the villa door early the next morning. Charlie opened the door and invited him in. Finley was making a pot of tea, while Whitt was getting fresh mugs down from the cabinet. None of them looked like they had gotten much sleep.

"Haven't the slightest. That is three murders in as many days," Finley solemnly stated. "We don't know when the bodyguard was done in, but it must have been the night before last. He was at lunch but not at dinner, as I recall."

"What have you found out?" Whitt looked up from arranging some breakfast rolls she'd ordered from room service and directed her question at Evans.

Before he could answer, there was a light tap on the door. Charlie went to open it. She had a feeling who it would be.

Cam hurried into the room after giving Charlie a wink and a lopsided smile. "The police are here. They brought in the big guns this time. Some inspector from Manila. That's why they are only getting here now. They've shut the place down and sequestered all the guests."

"I bet that went over real well with Miss International. I'm sure she's livid." Whitt snickered. "She probably doesn't have any place else to go, but she isn't used to having people telling her what to do."

"You called that one right. She was in the lobby hollering at the poor manager. Flores looks like death warmed over himself." Cam reached for the mug of steaming tea that Finley offered.

"Honey or calamansi?" Finley pushed the plate of calamansi limes and the honey bowl closer to Cam. "The poor man is probably worried to death about his reputation and his job. He tried so hard to keep all of this quiet, and now he has not just three deaths but possibly three murders on his hands."

"Maybe if he had allowed someone to help him when the spa attendant was killed, he might have saved himself the bother of the other two," Charlie considered.

"Do you think all of them are related?" Whitt asked. "I don't see the link."

Evans let Finley top off his tea. "Neither do I, but we know there must be one. I don't believe in coincidences."

"Let's go through what we know about each death—the timing, the cause, who was around," Whitt suggested. Finley reached into the drawer and pulled out a pad of paper and a pen.

"Sister of mine, do your thing." She passed the paper to Whitt, who always thought better when she was writing. In the past, her scribbling had been the key to understanding who among several suspects had the right mix of means, motive, and opportunity to move them from suspect to accused.

"Okay, with the first young woman, what was the cause of death and how long before we found her had she been dead?" Whitt had divided the paper into three columns.

Evans reoriented himself on the kitchen stool to face Whitt, who was sitting at the dining table. "The water would have confused the time of death, but as I recall, her neck had been broken."

"So, we're sure it wasn't drowning? Just made to look like it." Finley grabbed her mug and found herself a chair.

"The autopsy report indicated she had no water in her lungs," Cam confirmed.

"Did anyone see her with other staff or guests earlier that morning? We found her at around ten or so. Shortly after Charlie arrived," Whitt recalled.

"Not that anyone mentioned." Cam took the red bean danish Finley offered.

"If that's all we have on the first woman, let's move on to the bodyguard. When was he last seen?"

"At lunch, I think. Charlie, can you remember?" Whitt asked her friend.

Charlie shook her head and poured herself another cup of matcha tea.

"I think the whole contingent was at lunch." Charlie paused mid-thought.

Finley could see her mind working to reorder the events so they better fit reality.

Charlie corrected herself. "No, it was dinner when we last saw them. Remember, the kids got restless after they ate, and one of the bodyguards and all the nannies went with the children. The other guard stayed with the adults."

"Now that you say it, I do remember. Good catch." Finley turned to Whitt with a curious look. "And I also remember you talking about a python when we played the Murder Game. 'The woman in the blue caftan in the pool with a python.'"

Whitt's mouth dropped open. She sputtered before regaining her composure. "You don't think I had anything to do with Melinda's death! I was with you the whole time."

Finley laughed. "No, you goose. I was just thinking how easy it was to think up a scenario using a snake since we're in a jungle. The killer didn't have to get too creative."

"Apparently, someone agreed with you," Evans muttered.

Finley observed Evans. *He's frustrated, I can see. But how does any of this relate to Sanderford? Is he bumping off people now? And if so, why?*

Finley returned to the three real murders. "Before we move to Melinda, let's finish with the bodyguard."

"So, you all agree that both guards were at dinner and then they split up. Do you remember which one went with the kids?" Cam asked.

"Sorry, but I couldn't really tell them apart. Just big, built men in black with dark sunglasses on," Whitt declared.

"Yeah, I'm with Whitt. We were never formally introduced to any of the Pineda crew. The only thing that I recall is hearing a sound outside after we got back from our late-night tea session and were playing cards." Finley was trying hard to recall all the things that happened that night.

"You're right. We had seen Melinda and Arun fighting before he drove off." Whitt scrunched her eyes closed to replay the events of that evening. "And then Melinda went off with Ben sometime later."

"Noelle also left that night," Charlie reminded them.

"Wait, Noelle checked out? And Melinda was with Ben, not Arun?" Cam looked surprised. "Where was I when all of this was going on?"

"Probably tracking Sanderford and his crew. Which is what we are here for," Evans responded, the slight flexing of his mouth the only visible indication of peevishness.

"Which brings us back to how any of this is connected. And even if these murders are connected to each other, how are they connected to Sanderford?" Finley looked over at Whitt's pad. She wished they had a whiteboard. Whitt's paper had too many scribbles on it to make sense to anyone but Whitt.

"I'm still trying to tie things together, so details matter." Evans's gaze was hawklike. "Let's go back. You said you heard a sound the night the bodyguard was murdered."

"Yes, it was like a muffled scream. I thought it was an animal in the ravine since I didn't hear it again."

"What time was this?" Cam picked up the thread.

"Around midnight or later. I know it was late. We closed up the lounge bar and then sat up here playing poker and talking about Melinda and Arun and Ben," Finley replied.

"It was a real soap opera that night." Whitt leaned forward, her eyes fixed on Evans. "Why?"

"I suspect what you heard was the bodyguard being killed and thrown over the retaining wall. The time would be right."

"Thank goodness you didn't walk up on whoever it was in the middle of the crime." Cam glanced at Charlie.

"So have we covered the bodyguard?" Whitt looked at Cam and Evans. "What do we know about Melinda's death? We haven't heard anything since last night."

"You were there?" Cam was staring incredulously at Charlie now.

Charlie took another sip of her tea and calmly replied, "Yes, we were walking back from dinner and heard Marisol—she's one of the spa attendants—we heard her scream. We went over to the sauna, and then we saw Melinda."

"Describe it to me." Evans's brow knitted even closer together than before as he waited for someone to begin.

"When we got there, as Charlie said, there were three, no, four people near the door of the sauna. An older man and his wife and then a younger couple. The man told us what happened. His wife was looking after Marisol."

Evans continued his questioning. "How did you know there was a snake involved? Did you see it?"

"Initially the man said that reception and the snake handler had been called," Finley recounted. "Whitt asked why, and he moved aside so we could look into the sauna. The snake was wrapped around her."

"Was anyone else around?" Cam probed.

"No, just the other couple," Whitt responded.

"And Lilith," Charlie added matter-of-factly.

"Lilith? You saw her near the sauna?" Whitt almost rose from her chair to look at Charlie.

"Yes. She was near the studio when Cam and I came back from our run, and then she was hanging around when Melinda and Ben headed to the sauna. She had to have seen them."

"But what about when you found Melinda? Did you see her then?" Evans asked.

"Yes, she was standing on the path, a bit away from where we all were gathered."

"Was she by herself?" Evans twisted his mouth and pulled at his lip, seemingly in thought.

Charlie nodded. "After a couple of minutes, she walked off down the path to the lower villas. I thought it was a little strange her being out so late, alone."

As Finley, Whitt, and Charlie approached the dining room later that morning, they saw clusters of police officers scattered about the reception pavilion and spa center. Men in white coveralls with plastic bags followed behind other police with cameras. Mr. Flores, the manager, was beside himself trying to keep the throngs from trampling the plantings.

With spa services closed and that section of the property being combed for clues, guests had few places to go. As a result, many just sat in the dining area, sipping tea and sharing information on the murder in the sauna.

"Do you think the boyfriend did it? I saw him last night. He didn't look like the kind who would kill his girlfriend. At least not like that!" Finley heard an older British man in khaki shorts and a sun hat say.

"The police have that Bollywood actor and the yoga teacher behind closed doors," another guest shared as the women found their way to a cleared table.

"The police are moving pretty quickly to narrow down suspects," Finley said as she gave the menu a quick glance before closing it and looking up for the waiter.

"I guess they have to. They are on the verge of having a serial killer on their hands if they don't close in on a suspect," Charlie conjectured.

"You've got a point." Whitt closed her eyes and made a random selection from the menu.

"Is that how you decide on breakfast? What if you end up with turkey gizzards or offal?"

"That's not likely to happen here. The worst I can end up with is tofu sausage or bulgur wheat porridge." Whitt wrinkled her nose at the prospect of the latter gelatinous breakfast bowl. "Thank goodness I ended up with eggless buckwheat pancakes."

Charlie took a gulp of her kelp smoothie, making a face as she swallowed the green liquid before she brought them back to the murders. "Do you really think Arun did it? I know he was hanging around, but I can't imagine either him or Ben carrying in a snake so it could kill her. Where would they have gotten the snake? It would have taken some planning."

"There are so many things that don't make sense about any of the three deaths. And until someone can connect them for us, I think we need to think of each one separately," Finley said.

Whitt shook her head. "But you know these aren't isolated incidents. This is just too big a coincidence."

"Agreed, but the golden thread isn't going to become visible until we uncover some of the hidden elements of each of these murders." Finley sighed. "And that still doesn't help us with figuring out what Sanderford is up to."

Finley was just about to take a bite of eggless veggie omelet when she caught a glimpse of Arun, and then Ben, being led to awaiting police cars. "So much for our vote of confidence in those two. The police clearly think otherwise."

11

FINLEY, WHITT, AND CHARLIE TOOK their time over breakfast. Like the rest of the guests, they had nowhere in particular to go.

"Both pools are going to be really crowded. Want to take a walk instead?" Whitt suggested as they prepared to leave the table.

"Sure. Since we have the time, maybe we can take the ridge path that Charlie ran yesterday. Not sure that I want to walk all the way to the lookout, but we can start out that way."

"There are benches along the way as well as earlier turnoffs, so we don't have to commit now to doing the whole trail."

Whitt gave a thumbs-up. "Works for me. Let me change shoes and we can head out."

The sun was high in the sky by the time the women were ready for their walk. The thick canopy of the jungle shaded them as they headed toward the ridge path. Once there, a row of palm trees provided protection against the heat.

The women walked slowly, almost laboriously, their minds heavy with bits of information that failed to weave into any plausible plot. The police were concentrating on the murder of Melinda since it was where the Summit management wanted them to focus—and the Summit owners had the clout to influence the direction of the investigation. The police had latched onto Ben. But if Ben was the killer, then what was his connection to the dead bodyguard and the poor, almost forgotten spa attendant?

"Was there any indication that Ben knew the bodyguard?" Whitt asked as they passed the five-kilometer mark. "Let's assume for the moment that he knew the spa attendant since he worked in the yoga studio. It may be a fallacious assumption, but let's go with it for now."

Finley threw up her hands in surrender. "Fine. It narrows the number of killers we have to find."

"As far as I could see, Ben didn't know the guard. He was with Evans, Cam—and Lilith or Melinda if he wasn't at the studio," Charlie observed.

"Well, if he were doing something illegal, we wouldn't have seen him associating with his contacts, right? We wouldn't have seen the who or when," Whitt conjectured. Finley could tell Whitt wasn't convinced even as she threw out the scenario.

"Okay, so if Ben were doing something illegal that involved the dead guard, what was it that would have included Melinda?" Finley asked, trying to find the thread that tied Ben to the three murders.

"Maybe it didn't involve Melinda, per se. Maybe she heard or saw something she shouldn't have when she was with him," Whitt countered.

"But what?" Charlie walked toward the bench and sat down. "I am not seeing the motive besides being in the wrong place at the wrong time. That can't be true for all three victims, can it?"

"That would make for a pretty random crime, now that you say it out loud," Whitt agreed.

"Let's assume that Ben committed the first murder—" Finley started.

"But why?" Whitt interrupted.

"I don't know why. Let's set aside the motives and just say Ben killed them all. How does it tie to Sanderford? I refuse to believe that three people are dead and the master criminal that has Interpol tracking him isn't somehow involved," Finley declared, looking to the other two for an answer.

"Agreed on the Sanderford connection. But I want to throw something else out before we get to Sanderford. What about Noelle?" Charlie asked.

Whitt looked confused. "What about her?"

"Since we are throwing out possible suspects, we might not want to take her off the list just yet." Charlie bent down and retied her shoe.

Finley's face lit up as she considered Charlie's suggestion. "So, what you're saying is just because Noelle left, she's just out of sight, not out of the picture? Interesting."

"But wait—Melinda and Noelle were friends. They greeted each other like long-lost pals a few days ago." Whitt stroked her bottom lip in thought, her forehead crinkling.

"And Arun and Melinda were lovers less than twenty-four hours ago, too. Things change. And as we have seen, pretty quickly," Finley countered with a smile and a tilt of her head. *All may not be as it seems. We are going to have to delve deeper,* Finley concluded.

Whitt and Charlie were silent for several minutes before Whitt got up from the bench and shrugged. "But we still don't have motive. For any of them. And I haven't a clue how Mark is involved. I agree that Sanderford probably is connected, but I don't know how."

"Maybe a cup of tea will help us think more clearly," Charlie suggested. "Want to head back or walk a little further?"

"I'm ready to head back. Ten kilometers is more than enough for me," Whitt said.

Miss International was in the lobby when Finley, Charlie, and Whitt returned from their walk. She was in rare form. She had cornered Mr. Flores behind the reception desk and was jabbing a carefully manicured finger into his chest.

"I don't care what the police say. I am not staying here one minute longer. *You* are responsible for the chaos here at the Summit! *You* are responsible for interrupting my holiday! *You* are responsible for me not having a bodyguard here, having to choose between my protection and that of my family!"

Whitt stopped short as the threesome reached the reception pavilion. "She can't be serious. Is she really accusing him of being responsible for the death of her bodyguard?"

"She isn't concerned about his death. She is concerned that she doesn't have protection because he is dead. There is a difference," Finley explained.

Charlie simply shook her head. "That's sad. That's really sad."

The women watched as Angela Pineda continued, "I know people in *very* high places in the Philippines. This is not going to go without some serious complaint to *your* boss and *his* boss, too."

The manager tried to escape her pointed fingernails but failed. She continued to poke his chest to emphasize each word. The arrival of a police car was the only thing that saved him from being impaled by Miss International's talons.

"Mr. Flores, may I have a word?" The inspector from Manila smiled wryly at the scene that he had walked in on. Flores shuffled to the inspector's side, away from Angela Pineda's reach.

Finley strained to hear the conversation without appearing too obvious. While she didn't catch the full conversation, she heard "no one is to leave" clearly enough, reinforcing the message that the hotel manager had apparently been trying to convey to Miss International.

While they watched, the inspector greeted Angela. "Mrs. Pineda, I am sorry to have to inconvenience you, but this is a murder investigation, one that involves a member of your staff. I am sure you want to be sure that the full force of the law is brought to bear on the perpetrator of this heinous crime, ma'am."

Miss International drew back as the inspector took her hand in his and delivered his heartfelt message. Her face softened as he continued to work his charms on her.

"I do hope you understand and can endure this disruption in your busy schedule as we try to solve these horrible murders." The inspector brought her hand to his lips. "Please accept my admiration for your courage and perseverance during this difficult time."

After the inspector had left down the path toward the spa center, a trail of officers following in his wake, Angela Pineda stood transfixed, her hand still midair.

"Mrs. Pineda, I hope you and your family will accept a basket of fruit on the house for your trials," Mr. Flores said, taking the hand that still hadn't been dropped.

At his touch, Miss International snatched back her hand and stormed off. "I am not finished with you yet!"

Flores followed her exit until she rounded the corner. Then he smirked and threw up his hand dismissively before barking orders at the staff members who had retreated behind a screen during his dressing down.

"Well, isn't that special, as the Church Lady would say?" Whitt pursed her lips in imitation of the *SNL* character before turning and heading toward the lounge. "That calls for a drink. God, I wish there was bourbon!"

While they waited for a waiter to take their orders in the now-empty lounge bar, the three women were silent, processing what had just occurred as well as the details surrounding the murders. Whitt bit one of her fingernails as she thought while Finley fingered the beads of her necklace. Charlie stared in front of her and sighed.

"Who do you think did it?" It was Whitt who spoke first.

"Did what? The three murders?" Finley looked puzzled. "Isn't that what we have been talking about for the last couple of hours?"

"Yes, but we've been trying to analyze it. Let's play the Murder Game and see what we come up with."

Finley chuckled. "You and that blasted game! Well, since nothing else seems to be working. All right—who's the victim?"

"A young woman who worked at the spa."

"How'd she die?"

"Broken neck."

"What else do we know?"

"Not much. She was found away from the main buildings, floating in the water."

"So not drowned. Was there any indication that she was carried or dragged there?"

"None that were evident. She could have been killed elsewhere and dumped there or she could have met with her death there."

"Any boyfriend or lover that might have done it?"

"Nothing that was uncovered."

Charlie listened to the exchange, following the volley of facts and conjecture back and forth between the two sisters.

"She was killed to silence her. She wasn't part of the main plot," Charlie announced without fanfare. She looked up to find Finley and Whitt looking at her, both with congratulatory smiles on their faces.

"Then we all agree," Whitt concluded. "One down, two to go."

Mark Sanderford and his entourage were at lunch, occupying the tables tucked in the corner. Anya, Lorena, and Teresa were lined up facing Mark, Danny, and another man who Finley had seen before but couldn't recall being introduced to. As before, Mark sat facing the room, flanked by the large men who shadowed his every move.

"Could you live like that?" Whitt wondered out loud as she scanned the action in the Sanderford corner.

"Like what?" Charlie played with the faux pasta on her plate before venturing a bite.

"Surrounded by guards, always on alert." Whitt observed another man come in from the patio and whisper something in Sanderford's ear.

Sanderford's nostrils flared. The laughter and conversation at the table went quiet. The tension was palpable from across the room.

The three women held their breath, waiting for the man to erupt. Instead, he took a breath, pressed his palms to the table, and exhaled visibly. The messenger waited. Sanderford impatiently waved him away and smiled at the women in front of him. With that simple gesture, the conversation began again.

Whitt murmured, "Like that."

Finley sighed and took a forkful of salad. "When you adopt the lifestyle Sanderford has, you have to accept that it comes with a price tag."

As if on cue, Mark Sanderford stood and approached the table. "Hello, ladies. Hope you haven't been too troubled by all that's going on."

Finley noticed that he avoided the use of the word "murder." She wondered how much of a hand he'd had in those "goings-on." She never expected what he said next.

"The inspector has said that we can't leave the island for the time being, but he has allowed us some freedom. This place is going to be dead—excuse the pun—until they wrap this up, so I have invited a few guests over to my boat tomorrow."

"The inspector agreed to that?" Whitt questioned.

Sanderford smiled. "I can be persuasive when necessary. But there are conditions. We have to stay in local waters, and we have to be back by sunset."

He continued, "The girls are really hoping you'll come. I've invited a few others. Some prospective buyers. But pretty ladies—customers or not—are always welcome."

Before the women could answer, Anya came running over.

"Did you ask them?" She peered up at Mark, who put his arm around her shoulders and nodded. Anya squealed and turned to Charlie. "Are you going to come? Please. It'll be so much fun."

"I'll have to see what the others want to do," Charlie replied, which prompted Anya to launch another round of pleas.

"Baby, give them some room to decide," Mark crooned and squeezed her shoulder.

"Okay. I'll send over the details to you. Mark has even arranged a bus to take you to the boat. He thinks of everything!" Anya gushed as she headed back over to the table.

"I do hope you'll come." Mark sounded genuine. He smiled amiably and took his leave.

The threesome watched as the Sanderford crew prepared to leave. Mark caught Finley's eye and nodded as he slipped out the side door. Anya and the other women followed behind, waving as they went.

"What do you think that is about?" Finley asked when they had left.

"What he said. They're bored, and what do rich people do when they have nothing else to occupy them? They throw a party," Whitt replied.

"But we have had three murders!" Finley retorted.

"And he doesn't think they're his problem. If he ordered the murders, he isn't going to get upset, and if he didn't, he doesn't care," Whitt reasoned, and no one could fault her reasoning.

"Should we go?" Charlie's face said noncommittal. She wrinkled her nose even as she gave a half smile.

"I know it's so soon after Melinda's death, but we're out of ideas. Besides, we might learn something," Whitt suggested.

"That depends on who else is going. We could be stuck on a boat with a killer," Finley cautioned.

Charlie sighed. "Yeah, we might get more than we bargained for."

THE NEXT MORNING, AFTER BREAKFAST, a small bus was awaiting Finley, Whitt, and Charlie to take them down the hill to the harbor. Anya, Lorena, and Teresa were sitting just behind the driver, greeting guests as they boarded.

"Mark went to the boat to get everything ready. We had a girls' night last night. You should have come." Anya was in her perpetual good mood. She clapped her hands in delight as each new guest arrived.

Hunter and Jillian had already claimed one of the back benches when the threesome arrived. Another couple, an older man and his companion whom Finley and crew had seen but not yet met, were also seated in the middle of the bus. The three women sat behind Anya since she clearly wanted to talk.

"You are going to love the boat. There's a movie theater if you get bored sunning yourself. I can only take so much sun—I burn—so I'm under the sunshade most of the time." Anya pointed to her fair skin, which had more patches of pink than bronze.

Charlie smiled. "I'm with you. Good to know there is a place to hide from the sun."

"Do you have parties on the boat often?" Finley asked, giving her sister a side glance. Whitt gave Finley a complicit grin. *Might as well get info while we can,* Finley thought.

"Sometimes. Mark likes parties. But when there aren't parties, there are always fun new people on the boat for us to hang around with," Anya explained before turning to welcome the next guests.

Another young couple joined the group. Finley thought they were the same guests she had seen near the spa the night that Melinda died. She had spoken with them briefly at the pool. Brian and Yumiko Iverson. In their late 20s, he was in marketing, she in investments in Ho Chi Minh City. Seemed that they had moved there from London last year. They were taking a babymoon, having just learned they were expecting a sibling for their two-year-old son.

"Hi, so we meet again." Brian shook hands all around. Yumiko nodded. "Do you know Mark well? We just met him, but he seems a nice-enough chap."

"We just met him as well. It's kind of him to try to distract us after all that has happened," Finley said.

"Indeed. Really something. Do the police have any idea what happened? Are they calling it an accident? We haven't been hanging about much. Enjoying the quiet away from people before the baby-storm!"

"Are you expecting?" Whitt looked over at Yumiko. Finley realized neither Whitt nor Charlie had been there during their introductory meeting by the pool.

"Yes. Our second." Yumiko beamed. Before she could say more, Brian had pulled up pictures of their son to show Whitt and Charlie.

As the women finished looking at baby pictures, Cam and Evans mounted the bus stairs. Cam made a beeline for the empty seat beside Charlie. He introduced himself to Brian and Yumiko before settling back in his seat.

"I was hoping you'd be on this shindig. Maybe I won't be forced to spend my sunning time advising people on the proper way to do a squat!" Cam whispered as he sat down.

Evans dropped into the seat behind Finley and Whitt. "Ladies." He paused and raised one of his hawklike brows before whispering, "Should be interesting."

Before he could say more, Angela Pineda swanned onto the bus, her crew trotting along behind her. It was a smaller contingent than normal. The nannies and children stayed behind, as did her parents.

"Spanky pleaded so much, I just had to give in!" Miss International sashayed up the aisle, her designer caftan flowing, followed by her husband Spanky, the assistant, and her sister Rochelle.

"She must have left the bodyguard with the kids. Must think the assistant can handle any trouble. He's a big guy." Whitt looked up from a home design magazine when the entourage walked through.

"I think the assistant is here for her sister." Charlie cast an appraising glance at the strategic placement of the man's hand on Rochelle's lower back as he ushered her into a seat.

"Well, well." Finley looked puzzled. "I didn't see that coming, did you?"

Whitt smirked. "I told you so!" Cam and Evans just smiled wryly.

The Andersons were the last ones on the bus, grabbing a couple of seats toward the back. While the kids looked excited about the outing, Jamie and Lilith looked less enthused. Jamie seemed more distracted and flustered than usual. It took a couple of times before he heard his son's question about the choice of seats.

"I'll sit with you. Let your sister and your mother sit together," he said before directing his son into a seat behind his wife and daughter.

When Lilith removed her sunglasses and slipped them into her bag before sitting down, Finley could see her eyes were red and slightly puffy. Lilith diverted her eyes when Finley smiled a greeting. The sisters exchanged a knowing side glance.

The trip down the hill to the harbor took far less time than Finley had remembered when they'd headed up to the spa for the first time. Mark's "boat" was anchored at the far end of the harbor, away from much of the small-vessel tourist traffic. There were a few other yachts moored nearby but nothing to compare with the sleek 183-foot Westport triple-decker.

"I guess if you're going to broker yachts for a living, you might as well show off the top of the line," Whitt said as she took in the full majesty of the yacht on which they would be spending the day.

Finley watched Evans and Cam as they sized up the boat. She wondered whether they had known in advance the type of boat he had and the layout. From what she knew of Evans, she was sure he had done his homework. She hung back as they exited.

"What's the plan of attack? What do you want us to do?"

"Besides look pretty?" Evans drew back as he delivered the comment, waiting for Finley's reaction.

To his surprise, Finley refrained from jabbing him with her sunglasses. Instead, she put the shades on, pulled her beach bag onto her shoulder, and slipped her hand through Evans's arm. She pulled him to her and whispered into his ear, "Besides look *very* pretty."

Evans gave her a lopsided grin. "Observe. Take in whatever you can as intelligence. We'll talk later. Do you have your camera?"

Finley patted the side of her bag as they walked up the gangplank.

"Welcome!" Mark was his usual charming self. "I am so glad you came. Anya is just bursting."

Evans, in his role as the super-wealthy Thatcher Hayes, launched the opening gambit. "Danny said this boat was a beauty, but he didn't do her justice. Do you mind if we wander around?"

Mark shifted into sales mode. "Make yourselves at home. Be sure to drop in and let the captain walk you through what she can do. And I know Danny will take very good care of you!"

With that, Evans led Finley over to where Whitt and the others were standing.

"Done?" Cam asked as he handed Charlie a glass of champagne from the tray offered by a waiter.

"Done," Evans replied, passing Whitt and Finley their flutes.

"Then let's wander," Whitt suggested as she, Charlie, and Cam headed to the upper deck.

Before Evans could decide his preference of direction, Danny grabbed him by the arm. "Thatcher, Mark wanted me to be sure that you got a good look at the bridge."

"Finley, you're welcome to come, too," Evans/Thatcher called over his shoulder as Danny started the tour.

"Of course. The more the merrier." Danny redirected his attention to Finley. "Please join us."

"I may join you later. I'll just wander now. But thanks," Finley demurred.

Evans cut her a glance as he surrendered to Danny.

Finley waited until they were on the far side of the boat before she reached into her bag and pulled out her camera. She began with innocuous shots of the other boats in the harbor. There were several two-masted sailboats that she was sure Max would have loved to have boarded.

There was another superyacht that Finley assumed was Arun's, a trim eighty-footer with twin Jet Ski launches. She paused to imagine Melinda and Arun, only a week ago, going off together to explore the surrounding caves and coves along the Palawan coast. Now, from what she could see, no one was milling about, and all the curtains appeared drawn. It seemed even Arun's boat was in mourning for Melinda.

Finley redirected her attention out to sea. The water was calm, reflecting a cerulean sky that was dotted with a handful of billowy clouds, just enough to block the full force of the sun but not enough to spoil a day of swimming and sunning. Finley focused her lens on the bands of blue that stretched out beyond the harbor. Cyan, marine, electric, indigo, and navy. She was so focused on the palette of colors playing out before her that she didn't hear one of the guards slip up beside her.

"I'm sorry, ma'am, but no photos." Before he could finish, Mark called out.

"Yuri!" was all he said, with a shake of his head.

The man bowed slightly before taking his leave.

Finley turned to throw up a hand in thanks, but Mark was gone. *Wonder what that was about. My real question is why Mark is allowing me to take pictures, not why Yuri wanted to prohibit it.*

With permission granted, Finley began taking shots in earnest. She turned the camera back to the boat itself, snapping frames of the guests already lounging on the upper sundeck and lower aft platform. As she moved forward along the main deck, she was struck by how large the vessel was. *You could get lost in here and wouldn't be found for days.* The thought scared her a bit as she considered the series of recent deaths.

She wandered along the broad decking that led to the bridge, snapping as she went. The light refracting off the water danced across her lens, creating little patterns of light and color. She considered using a filter to cut the glare but liked the effect she was getting.

From her position on the bow, Finley could hear conversations coming from the bridge as well as the upper deck. She caught part of the conversation between Evans and the captain about the boat's capabilities.

Boring, she decided and redirected her ear to a rather strained conversation between Jillian and a man, whose voice she couldn't recognize.

". . . we can't do it here. There are too many people milling about. He'd have your head."

"You need to grow a backbone!" Jillian hissed. The rest of her comment was lost in the wind.

Finley walked farther out on the bow, turning as if to take a picture of the yacht from that angle. Through the viewfinder, she could catch only part of the man with whom Jillian was talking. Finley could see now, simply from the man's stature, that it wasn't Hunter. She continued clicking on the off chance that she captured enough of him for an identification.

"Having fun?" A slight man with dark, curly hair peered over the thick professor-like glasses resting on his nose. He eyed her camera. "Does Mark know that you have that?"

Finley nodded. "Yes. One of your guys—Yuri, is it?—warned me off, but Mark said it was okay. I'm a travel writer. It isn't often that you get to go out on one of these things. This is awesome!"

"It is a unique experience," the man acknowledged with an engaging grin. "I'm Efram, by the way. Mark's CFO. The mole in the hole so to speak. Fortunately, they do let me see daylight sometimes!"

Finley liked this man. She extended her hand. "Finley. I'm one of the guests at the spa. Along with my sister and a friend who are around here somewhere."

"First time at the Summit?"

Finley nodded again. "Not at all what I had expected. With the murders, I mean. I'm doing a story on high-end Asian spas. I don't know how my editor wants me to position the Summit. It's kind of hard to write around a murder, much less three."

"Three?" Efram steepled his dark brows. "I heard about the guest, but who were the others?"

"A young spa attendant and then Mrs. Pineda's bodyguard."

At the last bit of information, Efram frowned. "I can see now where you have a problem. Unfortunate, very unfortunate."

Finley decided it was a good time to change the subject. "But Mark made the best of a bad situation with this party. Really kind of him to host us."

"That's Mark's way," Efram said offhandedly.

"Have you worked for him long?"

"About ten, eleven years. I started as one of his accountants, and now I'm his CFO. But my mother still doesn't know what I do for a living. She keeps telling me I should go back to accounting!"

Finley chuckled. *Maybe you should listen to your mama and cut the risk. Mark's businesses are going to get you in big trouble one day*, she thought, but she said nothing.

"Have you been to the bridge? If not, you should swing by. It's quite impressive." Efram started toward the back stairs for the lower deck. "But the real show is in the theater. Come on. I'll show you the best part."

Finley slung her camera around her neck and followed the man down a set of spiral stairs to a hallway that split on either side of a massive movie theater, big enough to seat at least thirty people. Anya and Lorena were midway through *The Notebook*, talking to the screen so intently that they didn't notice Finley and Efram.

"It's something, isn't it?" Efram gushed. "Mark put it in last year to keep the girls quiet when we're underway. They get bored. I just work."

Finley smiled sympathetically before turning her attention to a long, narrow room with a series of large mounted monitors and ambient lighting. In front of the first two screens, Naomi and Eric sat in oversize BarcaLoungers deep into *Minecraft*, one of the popular video games. Finley wondered whether their parents knew what they were playing when she saw explosions illuminate Naomi's screen. She returned her attention to Efram, who was explaining something about the game room.

"Mark put it in for some of his friends who are esporters. They can spend days in here."

"Esporters?"

"Sorry. Professionals gamers." Efram laughed. "I had to learn the lingo, too. I still don't get the fun of it. Maybe I'm just too old."

Efram looked up to see Danny signal him over. "Excuse me."

Finley stood and peered over the shoulder of Naomi as she played some game that had teams preparing for battle. She tried to understand the object of the game, other than complete and utter annihilation of the enemy, but failed to see it.

"Interesting conversation?" Evans asked as he came behind her and replaced her half-empty glass of bubbly with a fresh one. He moved her out of the noise of the game room and into a lounge area.

"Thanks. And yes, it was indeed an interesting chat. Efram is the CFO and an engaging fellow. I would like him . . . if I didn't know what he did." The latter part of the comment she whispered.

"I know what you mean. Danny is one of the best salesmen I have seen in a long time. He lets you sell yourself. I might be in the market for a boat."

"Really?" Finley was intrigued. She couldn't tell from the look on Evans's face whether he was serious.

"Yes. I think Mr. Thatcher Hayes is seriously considering a purchase."

13

"**W**HAT ARE YOU TO DO with a boat this big?" Finley asked. She really was wondering what made someone dump millions of dollars into a superyacht like this one, besides ego.

Evans picked up the prompt and began to expound on all the reasons Thatcher wanted a yacht. "I don't think I need something this big, but it would be nice to take friends out on the water whenever I wanted. Now I have to charter, which requires planning."

"But it seems like so much upkeep."

"Maybe, but that's why you let the broker take care of the maintenance plan as well."

Finley could see Danny's reflection in the glass that separated the game room from the lounge where they were standing.

Evans/Thatcher continued, playing to his audience. "I want one big enough to do ocean voyages but not so big that it's a money pit."

"How big is that? I have no idea how big this one is."

"I would say this one is about a 170-footer. I am looking for something closer to the 80-foot mark. I don't need a superyacht. Quite honestly, I wouldn't know what to do with one."

Danny came over. "You hit it almost on the head. This boat is a 183-foot Westport tri-deck. It has the sundeck, the main deck—where we are now—and then a hull deck where most of the bedrooms are."

"I like the layout, but I don't want to bother with something this large. I need something that sleeps six to eight people and can accommodate a small crew."

"So, about ninety feet or so. Oceangoing? Short trips or long haul?" Danny led Evans/Thatcher and Finley to a seating area and signaled a staff member to refresh their champagne.

"Probably trips down to the Caribbean from the US or to Ibiza from London. I'd let a crew take it over on the ocean crossings." Evans/Thatcher smiled at Finley. "Although an ocean trip might be fun."

Danny concurred. "From the US to the continent is pretty easy, but I would get a transporter for the return leg. That northern crossing can be a bit rough."

Evans/Thatcher nodded. "Duly noted."

Danny turned to Finley. "Do you like sailing?"

"Haven't done much of it lately, but my husband and I do like it," Finley replied, referring to Max. However, Danny's quick glance at her finger and sly smile at Evans suggested that Danny had Finley coupled with Evans/Thatcher. The crooked grin on Evans's face said he caught the matchmaking, too.

"Well, I am sure we can find just the right vessel for you two."

"How much would it cost to add a few extra features?" Finley asked, looking up at Evans/Thatcher innocently.

"I do like letting her help me spend my money!" Evans/Thatcher decided to engage in Finley's fun.

"Depends on what you are interested in." Danny looked like he had seen this gambit before—a basic pleasure boat becomes a walking cash register with what seems to be a few minor tweaks.

"I like the aft sundeck—and the game room." Finley watched the slight quirk of Evans/Thatcher's eyebrow, the only indication that he acknowledged where her line of inquiry was headed.

"That's not an insignificant addition, ma'am, if you want one that looks like this." He inclined his head toward the elaborate setup that Finley had seen earlier.

"Really? It looks like a few high-end monitors and some easy chairs," Finley suggested, casting a glance at the game lounge with an offhanded shrug.

Danny laughed. "It may look that way, but Mark put that in for his gaming friends. They are diehards. They can sit there playing for hours, so the systems have to be able to handle that type of streaming. And the seats have to be ergonomically designed for the players to game for long periods of time."

"So how much would that run me if Thatch wanted, let's say, four to six stations in a setup like that?"

"Depending on the quality of equipment, it might run you an additional half million for a cozy four-stage unit. We put in one for a client that ran a couple mil. I won't begin to tell you what this one cost!"

"Good gracious, where does all that money go?" Finley sat wide-eyed as she slowly examined the gaming stations.

Danny rattled off all the cost factors. "Mainly the systems and electronics that are all back behind this to keep the games streaming for long periods of play. The satellites to connect you to tournaments around the world, the cooling systems so you don't overheat, all the licenses. There's a lot to consider."

"Do you still want it?" Evans/Thatcher nudged Finley slightly.

Finley looked up at Evans/Thatcher coyly. "It would be a nice alternative to bridge."

"Whatever you want," Evans/Thatcher's deep baritone replied.

"Thank you. I think I'll run along and find the other ladies." Both men rose slightly in their seats as Finley grabbed her bag and headed off in search of Charlie and Whitt.

She found them lounging by the pool across from Lilith and Jamie. The latter two had put a chaise between them upon which they had heaped beach bags. To a casual observer, it looked like a family stashing their outing gear. To those with a backstory like Finley, Whitt, and Charlie, it spoke volumes as to the state of things in Denmark.

"Enjoying your sunbathing?" Finley dropped her satchel onto a lounge chair with a fringed awning and addressed her sister and friend.

"Yes, I normally seek the shade, but the clouds have given me just enough cover for a bit of lounging. And what the clouds don't provide, the awning does." Charlie looked over her shades, a large sun hat still shielding her face.

"I've just been observing the War of the Roses." Whitt nodded toward the lounging couple as she pulled herself into a sitting position. "Guess he doesn't take well to being cuckolded."

Finley slid off her sundress to reveal a chic black one-shouldered maillot. She stretched herself out on her chaise and sighed.

Whitt gave her a side glance. "And what have you been up to?"

"Taking pictures—and contemplating the purchase of a boat. At least Thatcher is."

"Thatcher? Who's Thatch—?" Whitt was about to ask before she caught herself. "Oh really?"

Finley grinned before lowering her voice. "And Danny thinks Thatcher is buying it for me!"

"Why would he think that?" Charlie tilted her head and adjusted her hat to see Finley.

"Just the way we came in and something I said during my conversation with Thatcher and Danny." Finley smirked. "I don't know whether Danny thinks I'm his wife or his bit on the side."

Whitt and Charlie looked at each other, confused.

"You're going to have to explain all that when we get back to the room." Whitt shook her head and signaled for more champagne.

"What is it we're drinking? It's exceptionally good, but I can't place it," Finley said as she took a sip of the fresh pour of bubbly.

"It's because you have only had it a few times." Whitt took a sip and savored it on her tongue. "It's Churchill." She was referring to

Pol Roger Sir Winston Churchill, a fine champagne favored by the late prime minister and so named after him.

"Ah, that explains it. I could get used to this." Finley took another sip.

"You sound like David in Jaipur. Every place he went in the Rambagh Palace, he said, 'I could get used to this!'" Whitt snickered.

Finley turned to Charlie to give her some background. "This was when we were in Jaipur and stayed at a hotel that used to be the Prince of Rajasthan's home. It was really over the top. Both David and Max got extremely comfortable there."

"Was that your first taste of Churchill?" Whitt asked.

"It may have been. I have tasted so many phenomenal champagnes with you, I can't remember when I tasted what when." Finley complimented her sister's refined taste in champagnes and her penchant for ordering them whenever she traveled with Finley. She figured her sister's knowledge of wines had only grown since her marriage to David, who was a purveyor of ancient world wines from Georgia, Moldova, and the central European region.

"Well, it is clear that Sanderford buys this stuff by the caseload. My glass hasn't been empty this whole day."

It was nearing midafternoon. Lunch had been served just after one o'clock when the boat anchored somewhere in the Sulu Sea. The meal had been a sumptuous buffet of filet, shrimp, lobster, fish, and chicken with an assortment of vegetables, fruit, and grain sides laid out on banana leaves and palm fronds in exotic displays that were closer to art than food plating.

The Anderson kids, like most of the guests, had their meals brought to them where they were, in Naomi and her brother's case in the game room, much to the consternation of their father. Lilith hadn't moved more than a hand to raise her glass since she arrived.

"They are going to think this is the norm," Jamie groused to no one in particular after a rather lengthy rant about responsibility and adhering to one's values.

Whitt and Finley glanced up as he rose from his lounge chair and stomped off toward the bridge.

"That was a little awkward," Whitt said, looking around. "Where have the Miss International crew planted themselves?"

"I saw Rochelle and the assistant up front swimming. And I think Spanky was hanging near Danny. Probably hoping to talk him into financing the new boat that he wants. Angela will likely surface at dinner."

"In a new designer outfit while the rest of us sit there with sun-baked hair and the smell of seaweed on our skin," Whitt quipped.

"We can shower and change into something else. There is an outrageous number of rooms on this boat, according to Danny. I haven't been below yet." Finley pulled her awning forward and her beach towel over her legs. "In the meantime, I am going to snooze until dinner."

When she woke up sometime later, Cam and Evans/Thatcher had joined them, with Cam stretched out next to Charlie talking and Evans/Thatcher reclining beside Finley, his eyes closed. Whitt was in the middle, fast asleep, with her book across her tummy.

"Have a nice nap?" Evans/Thatcher asked without moving.

"I thought you were dozing."

"I was until I heard you move."

"All that spook training," Finley whispered. She saw an eyebrow move in response and a grin start to appear before quickly disappearing.

"Part of the job, yes."

"Did you buy a boat?"

"Almost."

"Almost. What does that mean?"

Finley sat up and looked over at the still-reclining hulk of a man beside her. His T-shirt was stretched across a broad expanse of chest that she could see was very well defined. She had known Evans for years, but his height and breadth never ceased to amaze her.

"I got you your game room, my dunk pool, an extra bedroom, and a couple of Jet Ski launches, which may delay delivery. I told Danny I would think it over. I'll add your sundeck when I talk to him next. Maybe he'll throw it in."

"And how much is that going to run you?"

Evans/Thatcher paused for effect. "Just under ten million."

Finley gasped at the price tag. "Good gracious! Where's all this money coming from?"

Evans/Thatcher opened an eye and smiled. "If I decide to move forward, I have sources."

"When did you tell him you would let him know? You're just playing him, right?"

"Told him I needed to talk to you." Evans/Thatcher turned to look at her. "You don't think Max would mind if I bought you a little something, do you?"

Finley laughed openly now. "I think we confused Danny on our relationship."

"Yes. He doesn't know what to make of it."

"Good. Let's keep it that way. What's next?"

Evans/Thatcher closed his eyes again. "We'll have to see."

When teatime arrived, Finley roused herself and went looking for a bathroom. All the coffee and champagne had gotten to her. As she headed downstairs to the hull deck, Finley saw Hunter pull Jillian into one of the open bedrooms and push the door. Through the half-closed door, Finley could hear the two arguing. As she got closer, Finley slowed her pace to catch some of the conversation.

"Where have you been? I've been looking all over for you," Hunter asked, his voice strained.

"About. On the bridge. In the game room, in the control room. Around. About. What do you need?"

Finley listened more intently at the mention of the control room. *What is she doing in there? That's not a place strangers go. If they even know where it is. Strange,* Finley thought as she continued to listen.

"I checked all those places. I didn't need anything in particular. I was just wondering where you had gotten to. You keep running off."

"Did you miss me?" Finley heard Jillian say suggestively before one of them pushed the door closed with a click.

Finley scurried past and toward the bathroom.

Dinner was, as expected, an elaborate affair, notwithstanding the fact that most, except Miss International, were in various mixes of swimsuit cover-ups, shorts, and sundresses. Mark made the rounds of the several tables that had been set for guests to dine, in white slacks and a navy linen shirt, his blond hair made even more golden by the day of sun. Waitstaff served the meal—filet mignon, giant prawn, a potato gratin, and fresh vegetables. The several vegetarians in the group dined on a vegan terrine with some sort of coulis.

As dessert and after-dinner drinks were served, Mark took the floor.

"I do hope you have enjoyed your outing. We had a great time hosting you, didn't we ladies?"

Anya squealed her delight while Lorena and Teresa nodded. Finley saw the bodyguards move to position themselves on either side of the room. From the shift in Evans's and Cam's body position, she knew they had seen it, too. She wondered whether they were armed.

"I wanted to take this opportunity to say good night and goodbye. The kind inspector has sent word that a suspect has been taken into custody and that we are free to leave the Summit. As such, my team and I will be leaving the day after tomorrow."

Spanky let out an audible sigh of disappointment that was quickly shushed by Angela.

Mark gave Spanky an appreciative smile. "Several of you have indicated an interest in transacting with us. We will of course try our best to accommodate that interest before we depart. In the meantime, enjoy the rest of your evening. The bus will be here in an hour to take you back to the Summit. Good evening."

Finley leaned over to Evans/Thatcher. "What does that mean for you?"

"We need to get back to the spa and decide." Evans/Thatcher did not look pleased.

14

THE RIDE BACK UP THE hill from the harbor was quiet without the Sanderford ladies, namely Anya, to set the tone. The Anderson adults still weren't talking to each other, and the kids were back into their video games. Miss International and her entourage were deep in thought. Every time Spanky tried to talk to Angela, she raised her hand to silence him. After the third time, he gave up. The older couple that Finley had not known had at some point in the evening introduced themselves as Aussie business contacts of Mark's, which caught Cam and Evan's attention. They were now asleep after a day in the sun, as were the babymooners.

As for Finley and her group, they too were each in their own heads. Whitt's lips were pursed as she researched something on her cell phone, which had been returned to her for the day trip on the boat. Charlie and Cam sat side by side, Charlie looking out the window as Cam slept. Evans had taken a seat to himself in front of the sisters this time. Finley watched as his brows knitted themselves closer and closer together.

He only has one day to figure out what Sanderford is up to and how to stop it. And that doesn't take into consideration determining whether any of the Sanderford business is connected to the three murders, Finley knew.

"Can we swing by your room in thirty minutes? We won't have cell phones to coordinate schedules once we get to reception," Evans whispered as they neared the front gate of the Summit.

Finley nodded. Whitt was focused on getting the last of her research done by the time reception gathered their phones again.

"Maybe I just won't give them mine!" Whitt said defiantly as the bus drew to a stop.

"You still won't have internet," Finley reminded her.

Whitt sighed and let the other guests exit as she continued reading something on her screen. "I think I'll remember most of it."

"Most of what?" Finley asked as she dropped her phone into the basket held by Dalisay.

"I'll tell you later." Whitt smiled at the receptionist and headed toward the villa.

When they got to the room, each of the women headed for the showers. Finley was the first one out. Her short hair was easy to wash and made for quick work in the shower. There were times when she could almost beat Max in efficient use of morning bathroom time. David and Whitt were another story. Finley knew that Cam and Evans would have arrived at the Blake sisters' villa long before Whitt would have finished her shower. What Whitt did in the shower that took that long Finley had never figured out.

Finley was on the phone ordering tea and snacks when Cam and Evans knocked. Charlie, who like Finley had taken only twenty minutes to shower and dress, answered the door.

"Do you have it all figured out?" Cam joked when they walked in. He gave Charlie a wink that made her blush.

"Why don't you guys grab a seat. Finley is ordering some tea. Whitt will be out in a moment." Charlie led the way into the sitting room and flopped on the sofa. Cam took the seat beside her while Evans paced.

"One day. One day is all we have," Evans said, more to himself than to anyone in the room. "I've already alerted Interpol that they are going to have to move fast or lose Sanderford. In the meantime, I need to figure out what I am going to do to trap him. I'm going to need help."

Finley was off the phone and reclining in one of the sleek club chairs. "Are you ready to buy that boat? It's the only thing that is going to slow them down, make them consider delaying a day. And once the money is paid, you have something to trace them with."

"You make a good point. We can buy ourselves time just by making a purchase." Evans stopped the pacing and pulled one of the dining room chairs into the sitting room.

Finley looked puzzled as he brought the chair over. There were other seats on the sofa and occasional chairs in the room.

Evans chuckled at her confusion. "I think better in straight-backed chairs. And I need to think this one through."

"While you're thinking, consider this." Whitt walked into the room, towel-drying her hair. In her sweatpants, she was rivaling Charlie for youngest-looking thirty-year-old on the planet. "They have been moving money from their arms sales for a long time."

"Meaning?" Finley asked.

"Meaning they're going to have a highly sophisticated, multi-layered process for laundering the money. Evans, Cam, can you run us through all the traditional ways for making it clean?"

Cam started listing the myriad channels large-scale operations might use to clean money coming through their system including any cash business like restaurants and car rentals or big-ticket businesses like real estate, art, rare books, and estate jewelry.

"As you guys probably know, more recently, big illegal operations have been using electronic channels to clean it, like crypto purchases and video gaming, this article was saying." Whitt claimed one of the chairs across from Charlie.

Finley nodded. "I recall hearing an NPR segment on this. They said in the Asian market, they can clean millions of dollars in just a few hours because of the advanced systems they have and the volume of gamers playing."

"Which means if we do use the boat purchase as the means to track the money, we have to make sure it is traceable. We can let it float for a while and then freeze it. But we have to do that fast," Cam said. "That's the thing with this guy. Every time we have tried to trace him using undercover dirty money, the money always disappears."

"So the question is how." Evans had grabbed a pad of paper and started laying out a plan of action.

"Efram said Mark had put in the gaming room for his friends, especially those in Asia. Maybe they are helping him clean the money he received through his other business dealings," Finley surmised.

"But none of us used their gaming stations, so do we even know what games they use to move it?" Cam raised the point that was gnawing at Finley.

"We didn't, but the Anderson kids did." Finley remembered that they had spent the whole day there, including lunch, much to their father's consternation.

"Okay, we'll talk to them tomorrow. In the meantime, we need to map the process, whatever game they use," Evans said.

Evans paused and reached in his pocket for a phone that had started to vibrate. He rose and went to the balcony to take the call. Within minutes he was back.

Whitt peppered him with questions. "What gives? How do you sneak in a phone and we can't? And how do you even get a connection?"

Evans gave her a grin that verged on a smirk. "Perks of the job. A satellite phone. Never leave home without it!"

Whitt harrumphed and shook her head.

"They have the money ready. Three million dollars for the first tranche. Let's hope that's all we need to catch him. All we have left in this operation is to understand the money flow." Evans returned to his seat.

"If you follow Whitt's line of thinking, Mark is going to mix it up—traditional and electronic, for sure. But I'd bet he has a bias toward electronic. I think it's through gaming. He's a modern guy. He moves fast and silently." Finley arranged the tea and snacks that had just arrived on the coffee table and began passing cups.

Whitt leaned forward and reached for Evans's paper and pen. "So, let's say your money comes into the system dirty. If this article is right, then he needs a few thousand players to buy things in the system if he is giving them money to distribute."

"Does he have that many friends?" Charlie asked.

"Friends can be easily bought," Cam replied, passing Charlie her cup of matcha tea.

"And what are they buying?" Evans looked puzzled. "I'm used to following large sums of money en masse. Tracking smurfing is tedious."

"The research said players buy treasure boxes with 'loot' that they can use in the various games. They use real money to buy the boxes."

Finley had picked up her tea and was walking slowly around the room. "Maybe, but let's work it from the other end. Let's say instead of hiring friends to buy loot to play the games in order to break up the payments, Mark sets up a store to buy the loot that anyone has won in a game."

"Then he doesn't have to worry about how many friends he has." Charlie had figured it out.

"But what does he do with all the loot he has bought?" Whitt asked. "He still wants real cash at the end of the day."

"There are legitimate companies that are always looking to replenish their loot inventory. So he factors it to brokers, gets his money—albeit at a discount—drops it in the bank, and moves on to his next deal," Finley surmised.

"He could do that very quickly." Evans was staring forward, his gaze hawklike.

"In a matter of hours," Whitt muttered.

"Sounds more than plausible," Cam shook his head.

Evans picked up the paper on which Whitt had drawn as Finley was talking. The pattern made a lot of sense and fit with the speed with which Sanderford appeared to make money disappear.

Evans looked at Finley, amazed. "How did you come to this?"

"I did a little reading, too. Since Cam first explained the process to me, I've been thinking about what would be necessary to run an operation like that. And then when I saw the gaming setup, I started researching on my phone. I think Whitt and I were doing the same thing."

"We just came at it from different ends. Like always." Whitt gave her sister a playful sneer.

"Now the question is how do we stop him?" Evans looked around at the group. "How do we shut him down?"

"I think that's where you and Cam come in. You have to figure out what he uses to buy and sell the loot. He must have a sizable network of these establishments." Finley poured herself more tea. "This is going to be a long night."

Evans smiled and caught Cam's eye. "Now you know why I read these ladies into my cases."

While Finley went to the phone to order more tea and snacks, Evans and the rest moved to the dining room table. Cam had pulled a small computer from his backpack and hot-linked it into the sat phone that Evans used. He snapped a picture of Whitt's flow map and pulled it up on his screen. From that picture, he then created a flowchart that he began to manipulate.

"A couple of essentials in whatever we do. We have to be sure the money's uniquely traceable, even after being broken up. And we need to be able to freeze it at any point in the process if this all starts going wrong. Mitigate our losses," Evans stressed.

"Once we decide on the games to be used, I can probably hack in and create a virus that attaches to the loot or games bought with dirty money," Cam said. "It won't stop the game, but maybe I'll just slow it down." He was typing away, his face getting more animated as he spoke. He turned and winked diabolically at Charlie, who laughed at his antics.

When Finley returned with the tea tray a few minutes later, the screen was filled with a detailed flow of the points of intervention, the nature of the tags that Interpol would put on the money, how it would be traced, and possible contingencies.

"Is that secure?" Finley asked as she poured out tea.

"Yes. Double encrypted. Just because it isn't a secure computer doesn't mean we can't create security." Cam grinned and nodded across at Evans. "These guys have to use whatever they can find wherever they are. We have to make it easy for them."

"Are we going to be shot at sunrise, working with you guys on this?" Whitt's voice had a slight catch in it. She had seen how nasty some of Evans's targets could get. She didn't want be on the receiving end of nasty this time.

"A knock at the door? An invitation for a strange rendezvous?" Evans spoke in a Charles Boyer voice, a French lilt flavoring the words. "No, you're safe, my dears. We would never put you in real danger."

"Not on purpose, at least," Finley muttered, recalling the times in their encounters with Evans that his targets had considered the sisters collateral damage.

Evans caught the comment and smiled. "Not on purpose."

"Look, it's going to take me a little while to set this up. I can just take it back to my room and work on it." Cam held up his flash drive to make the point.

"And have you drift off to sleep?" Evans challenged. "No, no, we can help keep you awake. Besides, what will happen to the ladies' reputations if we creep out of their rooms at one in the morning?"

"Will our reputations withstand it better if it's six instead?" Charlie asked.

Finley and her sister chortled. Leaving Cam and Charlie at the table, the other three took their teas back over to the sitting area.

"Well, while we are waiting for Cam to attack the cyberworld with viruses, perhaps we can help the poor inspector catch the

Summit serial killer." Whitt put one leg under her as she sat on the sofa.

"Serial killer suggests that it's the same person doing all the killing, and I'm not so sure it is." Evans took a sip of his tea. He looked up from the computer, brow raised, as if girded for pushback from the sisters.

"I was thinking the same. What if we are barking up the wrong tree, thinking it is one person and that person is related to Sanderford?" Finley said.

Whitt pursed her lips, unconvinced. "So you are saying the Summit just got caught in a weird tsunami of murders? I'm not buying it."

"Okay, let's see if we can convince you. That will be the proof the police will need to arrest the killer—or killers." Evans seemed to like the game they were about to play. Before he could start the questions, Finley interrupted.

"Who died?" Finley's eyes were locked on to Whitt. She was beginning another round of the Murder Game, and Whitt was a master at it. She might be able to weave the parts together where others had not.

"The young spa attendant."

"How did she die?"

"Broken neck. And then was put in the falls to make it look like drowning."

Evans watched the back and forth in silence, his head moving between Finley and Whitt like he was viewing a tennis match.

"Who do you suspect?"

"I don't really know."

"Don't think. Throw something out. Your gut reaction. Who did it?"

"Sanderford. More precisely, one of his goons."

"Okay, let's say Yuri. I don't know the other one's name. Why did he kill her?"

"She saw or heard something she shouldn't have."

"What?"

"I don't know."

"Don't think. Your gut."

"Something about his operations. A sale he was doing, a person he was meeting." Whitt paused. "That Aussie couple. They said they were one of Mark's contacts. Maybe it was something connected to that."

Evans leaned forward as if ready to speak, but Finley raised her hand to stop him. *She is on a roll. I want to tap everything she's thinking before I break her concentration,* Finley reasoned. Evans immediately caught her meaning and relaxed in the chair.

"Hold that. Now let's move on. Who died?"

"Angela's bodyguard."

"How was he killed?"

"Broken neck." Whitt sat up. "Two broken necks. I hadn't seen that before."

As Whitt spoke, the phone in Evans's pocket buzzed. He answered it, moving to the balcony again as he did. The conversation this time was considerably longer. Finley couldn't hear much of it, just lots of grunted yeses and nos. When he came back in, Evans paused at the door. He took a step in and squared his shoulders.

"We are going to have to move immediately. It appears Sanderford and his boys searched us up. The agency fed them enough information to make us credible. To bolster what was already out there." Evans smiled at Finley. "They created a little intrigue between the two of us. They'll take it down as soon as the deal is done, but you might want to tell Max in case anything leaks out."

Finley was wide-eyed. "I haven't even been able to tell Max that you are here. No phones, remember! You better have a whole lot of damage control ready when I see him in a couple days."

"Done. I promise!" Evans placed his hand on his heart.

He turned his attention to Cam. "Are you almost done with the trace? I need to send a message to Danny telling him it's a go. I'll do that early tomorrow, before breakfast. Let's see what he says."

15

DANNY RESPONDED IMMEDIATELY TO EVANS/THATCHER'S note. He suggested a conversation just after breakfast. When Finley, Whitt, and Charlie headed to the pool after their round of vegan buckwheat pancakes, Danny was just getting out of his car. He threw up his hand, said something to the driver, and started toward the three women.

"Lovely day, ladies. Headed to the pool or for a round of massages?" An attractive but hardly handsome man in his mid-thirties, he kept his short brown hair gelled in a style that created a glistening mountain range at the top of his head. His attire was always a step above the casual chic of his boss. Mark might have time to lounge, but Danny always looked like business. Today was no exception. His dark-navy trousers, white linen shirt, and navy- and white-flecked sports jacket made it clear he meant to close a deal.

"To the pool," Whitt replied. "You would have thought we got enough sun yesterday, but we're gluttons for punishment."

Danny chuckled and turned to Finley as Evans/Thatcher approached the group. "Will you be joining us?"

Evans/Thatcher answered for her. He took her elbow and directed her away from the others. "Of course, she will. Cam said he would look after Whitt and Charlie while we were away. You don't mind, do you? I want your opinion."

At that, Finley waved to the rest of the group, who were already making their way toward the pools.

"Now then, we can meet in my villa. There is a projection screen if you need it," Evans/Thatcher said.

The set of suites that made up Evans's compound reflected the wealth and stature of a man like Thatcher Hayes. Clustered around a richly landscaped center courtyard that housed the pool were a bedroom pagoda with three massive en suite bedrooms; an entertaining pagoda with a small movie theater and a juice bar as well as two sitting areas, a library, and a kitchen; and a business suite with a conference room, a separate office, and kitchenette. Finley imagined that Sanderford's compound must be a larger version of this configuration.

Evans/Thatcher led Danny and Finley to the large teak-paneled conference room.

"Can I offer you something to drink?" Looking pointedly at Finley, he asked, "Coffee, perhaps?"

Finley stared at him in surprise. "Real coffee? How did you manage that?"

Evans/Thatcher chuckled as he poured her a cup. "I thought you'd like my surprise."

Danny watched the exchange with interest. "I take it you've been missing your coffee during your stay."

"Missing it is an understatement. I think I almost OD'd on it on the boat yesterday. Efram was laughing at me. I think I had it hot, cold, iced, frapped, and affogatoed. You name it!"

"And that doesn't make you jittery? I would have been jumping out of my skin," Danny said as he took papers and folders from his briefcase.

"No, it makes her smile." Evans/Thatcher set a steaming mug in front of her and squeezed her shoulders as he passed. He mock whispered to Danny, "I'm a lucky man. It doesn't take much to make her smile."

"Just a yacht or two made to specification?" Danny smirked as he pulled out some materials from one of the folders. "We have a couple of options for you. Since we are short on time, I thought we could go through them quickly and see if any of these meet your needs."

Evans pulled the small sheath of pictures toward him and opened them so that both he and Finley could see them easily.

"With the addition of the pool, the Ferretti 860 that you were looking at wasn't going to work. We know you don't want anything too big, but we have a couple of options in the 110-foot range that might be a better fit. Not too over the top in looks, with good speed and easy handling on long hauls." Danny selected a couple of pictures from the pile and placed them on top.

"And all in the ten-mil range?" Evans picked up a glossy shot of a sleek multideck yacht with a built-in pool on one deck and multiple seating areas on the others.

"It'll be a little over with the game room and Jet Ski launches, but it has your extra bedroom and the pool. And it's under construction, so you can have the fittings and features done to your specifications with delivery in early 2024."

Evans pushed the pictures of the other yachts to the side and arrayed those of the Johnson Flybridge in front of Finley. "What do you think? Do you like it?"

Finley took in the shots in front of her. "How much to put in the game room?"

"About a half million, as I mentioned yesterday. We might be able to cut it a bit, but if you want top-end esport equipment, it's going to cost."

"If it's just for me, we can do without it, Thatch. That's a lot of money for some silly video games."

"But you want it!" Evans/Thatcher smiled and shook his head. "After she saw the one that Mark had, she couldn't stop talking about how much fun it would be to have one when she comes to visit. Is Mark a big gamer?"

"He plays a bit, but it's mainly for his friends who travel with him. And his Asian clients. Those are the big gamers!"

"Then she shall have her game room, too!" Evans/Thatcher stacked up the pictures. "What's the final price tag? And I know you're going to make me a good deal!"

Danny pulled out his computer and a handheld calculator and started punching in numbers with a smile aimed Finley's way. "Mark told me to make you a sweet one, so that's what we are going to try to do."

Finley noticed Danny's use of the royal "we" when he spoke. She wondered whether by using it, he felt absolved of all that he did in the name of Mark. She wondered what the business team did besides selling yachts. Were they also responsible for running the money laundry? She wished she understood more how the gaming side worked.

"Would I bother you if I asked a question?" Finley dropped her head, as if she were a little shy about interrupting.

Danny looked up briefly, realized the question was directed at him, and shook his head before going back to his number crunching. "No, not at all. Fire away."

"It's really going to be a stupid one." Finley sighed. "But here it goes. I was watching the kids play, and then I heard one of the guests talk about esporting, and people playing professionally, and it's not clicking for me. How?"

Danny finished with his numbers and stared at Finley. "And you want a game room?"

"Yeah, for people who want to play. I mean, people seem really into it. They look so happy when they're playing."

Danny sat back and took a gulp of his coffee. "For a gamer, the high comes in the journey up the ranks. For the professional, it's winning the tournaments at different levels of play and taking home the cash. For the amateur, it's staying in the game and collecting the 'loot.'"

"The loot? What's that?"

"Depends on the game, but it's the things you can win while you play that allow you to stay in the game or play at another level. We call it loot, but it's any sort of gaming enhancements. Sometimes it's in the game; sometimes you buy it. A lot of the time it comes in boxes so you never know what you've got that you can use until you open it. Which is what technically loot is."

"What fun! But what do you do with loot besides play more? What if you're tired of playing and want to go home?" Finley giggled. "Does it ever end?"

"Sure, you can cash out. Take your loot to the store and buy a prize or take cash."

"There are stores that take these loot things?" Finley laughed out loud. "Like can you take your loot to Gucci and use it like bitcoin to buy what you want? Not that I know how to use bitcoin either, but at least I've heard of that. This loot stuff I have never heard of before! It's wild, eh, Thatch?"

"You have to convert it, but there are a lot of stores out there in the online game world where you can buy things or just cash out. We own a few. Mainly so Mark can give his friends new games or enhancements. Just wait 'til you get your room. You're going to get sucked in."

Evans/Thatcher exhaled heavily. "So, I pull her out of the dark room and lose her to video games? From the frying pan into the fire!"

Finley reached over and touched Evans/Thatcher's hand. "It won't be that bad. But then again, you haven't heard the final price tag yet. Danny, tell us the damage!"

Danny slid a sheet with his calculations across the table. Evans/Thatcher caught the sheet and looked at the figure. A sly, crooked grin crossed his face as his eyes narrowed. Finley watched him as he ran his hand through his graying hair. She leaned over to see the price and swallowed hard. Ten point eight million dollars!

"Your best deal, Danny. Your *best* deal," was all Evans/Thatcher said, pushing the sheet back across the table.

Danny bit his lip, glanced up at Evans/Thatcher, and lowered his head over his calculator. His mouth twisted as he checked figures on his computer and then began entering them into his calculator. He struck through the number on the pricing sheet and slid it over to Evans/Thatcher again.

Without looking at it, Evans/Thatcher pushed the paper over to Finley. His eyes fixed on Danny. "Do you like it, Finley? *Really* like it?"

Finley looked at the sheet and saw the price, a significant discount from the earlier figure. She tilted her head slightly and caught Danny's eye. *I want to make him sweat. He didn't think that Evans would let me make the final decision. This is getting to be fun.* Her lips pulled up into a soft smile.

"May I borrow your pen, please?" Finley directed her question to Evans/Thatcher, but Danny obliged by passing her the Montblanc in his hand.

Her smile widened as the two men observed her cross through the new figure and reduce it to a solid nine point five million.

"Those other numbers looked a little messy just hanging there. This is a nice solid number that I think better reflects Mark's notion of a 'sweet deal.' What do you think, Thatch?"

Evans/Thatcher drew in a breath and let it out with a chuckle. "I like it. Can you start to like it, Danny?"

Danny reached for the sheet and grunted. "You better watch out for this one! She just got her game room pretty much free!"

"You're a dear, Danny. Thanks so much! You're going to make sure it's a really nice one, right?" Finley crooned.

"Top of the line. Mark said to give the lady what she wants, and you got it. Let me draw up this contract. Assuming Mark agrees, we can sign this evening. Why don't we send a car for you at, say, eight or so, and we can sign and celebrate?" Danny suggested.

Evans/Thatcher stood and walked Danny to the door. "I like the sound of that. Sign and celebrate."

"Can the others come, too? I've never been to a new yacht party before, and I know my sister and friend want to be there," Finley asked.

"Sure. The more the merrier. We'll see you at eight."

"What do you think they are doing?" Whitt had spread her towel across her legs in an effort to stop the morning sun from burning her before she tanned. She had switched into another bathing suit before breakfast, this one a deep dark-sage green number with a deep V. It wasn't her normal style, but she liked the color.

Besides the Anderson kids, who were in the pool, they were by themselves.

Cam glanced over at Charlie on the lounge chair beside him and whispered to Whitt, "Probably buying a boat."

"You're no fun!" Whitt waved him off. "I mean they've been in there a long time, and the clock is ticking."

"Have you found any more information that might clue us in on how Mark's gaming operation works?" Charlie asked.

"A bit, but short of hacking in, which I don't want to do unless it is the last option, not much," Cam admitted. "I have a training session with a guest in another thirty minutes; if they aren't out by then, I'll go in. Feel better?"

Whitt nodded and looked up to find Naomi and her brother hovering nearby. She had planned on interviewing them about how video gaming worked anyway, so she launched in. "Hi, how's it going? Did you guys have fun yesterday in the game room?"

Naomi, seemingly the bolder of the two, despite being younger, ignored her question and asked one of her own. "Are you guys cops?"

Cam, taken aback by the girl's directness, smiled and moved forward in his seat. "What makes you think that?"

"Just some stuff we heard you say just now, about the things on Mr. Sanderford's boat. Stuff in the game room."

"Yeah, we think we saw some stuff we weren't supposed to see."
Naomi's brother pretended to investigate something on his finger
that wasn't really there. He glanced up to see the adults' reaction.

"What sort of things did you see?" Whitt smiled and pulled
herself into a sitting position, her legs tucked under her. "And we're
not cops, so you can't get in trouble."

Naomi came and sat on the edge of her chaise and leaned in. "It
wasn't so much as in the game room as in the control room."

"Yeah, Mum said to stay out of the way, and so Jillian—she said
we could call her that—took us around and showed us all the stuff
on the bridge and how it made the boat go and all." Eric moved
forward as he spoke and stood near his sister.

"Well, while we were in the big computer room—"

"The control room."

"Yeah, the control room, Jillian hit some buttons, and a lot of
names and numbers came on the screen."

"We thought it was all part of a game at first, but then she
started acting weird," Eric said.

"I don't think we were supposed to see those, because as soon
as she saw what was on the screen, she shut it off and asked us if
we had seen anything. Like really cagey-like." Naomi moved her
shoulders like a cat on the prowl.

Her brother nodded. "We just played dumb and asked what
she was talking about. And then Naomi started asking gaming
questions."

"Jillian knows a lot about gaming. Somebody said she was a
ranked esporter."

"Anyway. So, she took us into the game room and started giving
us pointers in some of the really top games and stuff. Then we forgot
about it," her brother said.

Whitt looked over at Cam and Charlie, wondering where
the conversation was going. Short of going back to the boat and
hacking the control room, it was unlikely they were going to find
out what was on those screens that Jillian was hiding. All Whitt

knew thus far was that Jillian knew her way around the boat and probably was connected with Sanderford's operations. How, Whitt didn't know. Information that was potentially useful but not conclusive yet.

"Then what happened?" Charlie asked, looking first at Naomi and then at her brother.

They dropped their heads, casting side glances at each other, almost daring the other to go first.

"You won't get in trouble. I promise," Cam said.

Whitt wondered how he was going to deliver on that assurance, but his word seemed to have loosened the tongues of the pair.

"We went back to playing, and then later we went looking for our parents." Naomi had raised her head, but she was still wringing her hands.

"Yeah, they moved from the pool, and we didn't know where they were," her brother added.

Oh goodness. Their parents are involved in this. What do we say? Whitt exhaled and waited for the worst.

"We didn't mean to do it. Really! We were just looking for our parents." Naomi was close to tears.

Whitt reached out and pulled her closer. "It's all right. Just tell us what happened."

While Naomi collected herself, Eric went on. "We were near the front of the boat, looking around, and we heard two guys talking. About the girl that got killed."

"It was just when we got here that something happened to her." Naomi's eyes welled with tears. "We don't want to die. We didn't hear anything, really."

"You aren't going to die. We'll keep you safe," Cam assured the girl. "What did you hear?"

"That's pretty much it. They said she heard too much and so they killed her," Eric replied.

"When we heard that, we stopped listening and went back the other way," Naomi said. "We didn't dare tell our parents, but then we heard you talking, and we thought maybe you had heard the same thing. We were scared."

"It will be all right." Cam looked over the girl's head at Whitt. "Do you know which of the men were talking?"

Eric shook his head. "We couldn't see them. Just hear them."

"Okay. Thank you for telling us. We'll make sure the information gets to the right authorities." Cam shook Eric's hand and patted Naomi's arm as she stood to go. "We won't let anyone know where we got the information. No one will know what you told us. All right?"

Naomi and her brother nodded vigorously, glanced at each other, and headed back to the pool.

Whitt, Cam, and Charlie waited until they had swum to the far end of the pool before they resumed the conversation.

"Well, that didn't go in the direction I had thought it might," Whitt conceded.

"Where did you think it would go?" Charlie asked.

"To involve their parents! This makes it a lot easier. It's likely Sanderford had the girl killed because she was a risk. Pretty straight-forward." Whitt readjusted the towel and leaned back.

"But how do the other murders fit in, now that you have that one out of the way?" Cam asked.

"I'm not sure I do. Except for the broken neck, I don't know how Miss International's bodyguard is connected to Sanderford—or anyone else at the Summit, for that matter," Whitt admitted.

Charlie shook her head. "The one that has me really baffled is Melinda's death. We know now the connection of the spa attendant to Sanderford. I wonder if the Pineda's bodyguard also heard or saw something that he wasn't supposed to and had his neck broken. But what could Melinda have done that warranted that kind of death?"

Cam touched Charlie's hand gently. "You have a point. The other murders were short and sweet. A broken neck. Why was this one different, if all the murders were done by Sanderford's boys?"

There was a long pause in the conversation. Whitt opened her eyes to find both Charlie and Cam looking at her for the answer.

"Well, don't look at me! Maybe Evans is right and there is more than one murderer running around."

EVANS ARRIVED AT THE BLAKE villa shortly after Finley. Cam, Whitt, and Charlie were already there when Finley walked in.

Whitt was on the phone ordering tea and some sort of vegan cheesecake that she knew was made with tofu but had convinced herself tasted like the real thing.

Whitt placed the phone in the cradle as soon as Finley hit the threshold. "Where have you been? Does it take that long to buy a yacht?"

"With Thatcher! Where else?" Finley left the door cracked so Evans could get in. She dropped her satchel and sank into the cushions of the sofa. "I'm exhausted!"

"All that playacting tired you out?" Evans said as he walked in and closed the door behind him. He checked through the peephole to be sure he hadn't been followed before moving to the sliding doors to the pool and balcony to peer out.

Whitt observed him as he made his check. "Why are you checking around? You don't think they bought it?"

"Oh, they bought it, all right. Your sister here was brilliant. She toyed with Danny—and me—and got just what she wanted at a price that Danny wasn't sure how he had agreed to!" Evans pulled out a dining chair and sat down.

"Okay, fill us in. What happened?" Cam asked.

"We bought a bigger boat at a lesser price, that's what. And all because of this woman's negotiating skills." Evans chuckled.

"Too bad you can't keep it," Whitt reminded him.

Evans sighed. "True, but it was fun acting like I could."

"Now that we know the fun part, what else did you learn?" Cam crossed his arms waiting for the answer.

"That Mark doesn't play, but he lets his clients, particularly those in Asia, play a lot. Whitt will probably tell you that the Asian market for high-stakes gaming is probably the largest in the world," Finley said.

"And with Finley's skillful probing, Danny revealed that Sanderford owns several of those online gaming stores where people can buy and sell loot and other things for the games." Evans gave Finley a congratulatory nod.

"How did he let that slip?" Whitt wondered.

"He made it sound like it was a legitimate business, like their stores were just like all the others out there," Finley responded.

"But we know that isn't true." Charlie answered the door and let the waiter with the tea in. She waited until he left before continuing. "Did they say how many or mention the names of these online stores?"

"No, but I don't think it matters, now that I think of it. The money has been tagged with the virus so we can see where it goes and in what quantities." Finley got up and poured herself a cup of tea before passing the pot to Charlie. "I'm going to venture a guess as to what you will see."

Evans straightened in his chair and gave Finley a quizzical look. "Enlighten us."

"I think Sanderford may be hiding his laundry behind a clean business—like the gaming stores, but we don't know which one. Tracking the clean money will help you find out." Finley gave Evans a satisfied smile.

"Walk me through that again. I'm confused." Whitt twisted her mouth and closed one eye as Finley spoke.

"The questions that have been bugging me are one, how the dirty money disappears so quickly, and two, how you are going to use the clean money to track the dirty. That is, what is going to go on behind the scenes to tie the clean money to the dirty."

"Okay, keep going," Cam encouraged.

"I suspect that Efram is going to buy another gaming store with the clean money. Danny said they had a few. Then he is going to transfer it to a 'pseudo buyer,' namely a shell company that Mark will also own, which will take all of his inventory. With the dirty money cleaned in the lump-sum inventory sale, the 'buyer' can now take his time to sell the merch in the open market for real money."

"And if, as they say, the swap for currency can be done in a few hours, there is nothing dirty left for the authorities to find." Whitt shook her head at the ingeniousness of the operation.

"With the viral tracker that Cam put in, though, for the first time, you'll be able to trace it down to the last crumb," Finley added.

"Smart. Very smart." Cam nodded, an admiring smile gracing his lips.

"Well, we'll get to see soon enough. We're invited at eight this evening for the signing and celebration of our yacht purchase. I suspect they will move the money tomorrow once they are in international waters," Evans said.

"I didn't think about that." Whitt cut herself a piece of cheesecake, looking at Finley with surprise.

"What?" Finley was puzzled.

"That they would wait until they were far enough offshore before they did anything potentially illegal." Whitt laughed. "Guess they have heard about jails in the Philippines."

"Once the contract is signed, I'll wire three million into the account Danny gave me. And then the games begin." Evans sipped on his tea, seeming deep in thought.

"To confuse them if they also use trackers, I'm planning to use one of the Anderson kids' avatars to activate the viral trace so that as soon as it starts to move, we can follow it," Cam said.

Evans took the cheesecake Charlie offered him. "What else did you learn from the Anderson kids, if anything?"

Whitt could barely contain herself. She had just taken a mouthful of cheesecake and was fluttering her hand as if to will herself to chew more quickly.

"They say Jillian is involved in this somehow!" she blurted out, even as she swallowed the last bit of cheesecake. "We got so focused on your morning, we forgot to tell you about ours."

Finley looked at her sister and passed her a napkin. "Jillian? I know she's a gamer, but what role would she play in this?"

"Do you think she is the one laundering the funds for Sanderford?" Evans asked.

"I assumed it would be Efram, but maybe Mark keeps his hands clean by passing the risk over to a third party like Jillian." Finley shrugged.

"What exactly did the kids say?" Evans's eyes became hooded as his eyes narrowed.

Cam turned to Whitt and Charlie.

"They came to us because they were afraid they would get in trouble," Charlie explained. "They thought we were the police."

"Yeah, they said Jillian was showing them around the control room, and she accidentally hit a button that pulled things up on the screen that she didn't want them to see. They said she started acting weird," Cam added.

"Did they say what it was that they saw?" Finley was curious about what could get that sort of reaction from Jillian, who seemed like a cool cookie.

"A lot of names and numbers, according to Eric." Whitt put her plate down and sat back. "Jillian tried to make light of it. But that wasn't the best of what they said."

"What could be better than adding another suspect in this tangled web of intrigue?" Finley said in her best Alfred Hitchcock voice, rubbing her hands together like a villain.

"That someone on that boat yesterday admitted to killing the spa attendant." Whitt smiled back, her brows steepled.

"What?" Evans leaned forward in his seat. "Someone came right out and admitted to murder?"

"Who was it?" Finley shook her head in disbelief. "It wasn't Sanderford, was it?"

"No, the kids didn't see who was talking, but they said it was two men. When they heard that they had killed her because she knew too much, they stopped listening and skedaddled," Whitt said.

"Smart move. Who do you think it was?" Finley mentally scanned the list of suspects.

"Probably the bodyguards. Was there anything that tied them to the death of the other guard?" Evans was starting to pace now.

"The only thing I found on the guards was that they had been members of rival gangs years ago. Not much."

"I still say this all rolls back to Sanderford and his crew. We need to solidify the connections. The hardest one is Melinda's murder. If we can figure that connection out— assuming there is one— we'll have things wrapped up. But that's a big if." Evans paused his pacing to make the point.

"Well, we seem to have gotten farther than the police in solving these murders. They still are holding the wrong guys. Poor Ben— and Arun," Cam muttered.

"Look, Cam and I have some work we need to do before this evening. The car will come for us at eight. I suspect there will be an abundance of champagne, so line your stomachs accordingly," Evans warned.

"Mr. Hayes, you should know that a fine champagne will never give you a bad head or a turbulent tummy. Whatever have you been drinking?" Whitt teased in her mama's most refined southern accent.

Evans bowed to the ladies as he stood to leave. "My apologies, Ms. Blake. I forgot that you will only drink the finest of vintages, as I suspect will Mark Sanderford. We will ring for you a bit before eight."

"Are you guys going to be hungry for lunch?" Whitt asked as she, Finley, and Charlie cleared the teacups from the sitting room.

"Not really. That cheesecake was surprisingly good," Charlie said.

"I'll be fine until dinner. I think I am going to take a power nap and then head to the pool." Finley yawned. "We'll need to be alert for this evening. And besides, this is our last day here."

"You're right. I have been so focused on all the stuff with Sanderford and the murders that I forgot we head down the hill tomorrow. Maybe I'll fit in another massage while you are at the pool. What do you say, Charlie?"

"I would be up for another massage if we can book it."

"That does it, then. Nap and then a massage."

When Finley woke from her nap, her sister and Charlie had already headed to the spa center for their massages. Finley took her time pulling on her swimsuit, a red one-piece with a scoop neckline and a plunging back. *The better for sunning,* she thought.

She headed off for the pool, debating between the salt pool and the chlorinated one. In the end, the salt pool won out. As she walked up, the only other people in the area were a couple who looked like newlyweds, and they were packing up to leave.

Finley laid out her towel, grabbed her book, and settled in for a relaxing few hours before she too needed to clean up for dinner and prepare for the rendezvous on the Sanderford yacht. She had barely read the first paragraph of *Nora* when she heard her name.

"Finley?" It was Arun Mehta. The actor had been released by the police; Ben had not. He was rolling a large suitcase toward reception.

"Yes. Arun. I haven't seen you around the grounds. We are all so sorry about Melinda. Such a shock." Finley paused. "Such a loss."

"Thank you. I am still in shock myself." He looked down at the suitcase he was pulling. "I came to collect the rest of our things. Got everything but her phone. I couldn't find it."

"Didn't she leave her phone at the desk?" Finley wondered how she had gotten around the "no phone" rule.

He gave a half smile. "The regulars at the Summit know to bring a dummy phone to leave at the desk and hold on to their own. They just keep them out of sight. Melinda's is missing."

"I'm sure it will turn up somewhere among her things."

"You're probably right. It just had a few pictures . . ." His voice trailed off. He picked up the conversation on another train of thought. "I'm heading back to Mumbai. I can't stay here."

"I understand." Finley was afraid to ask about the movie. His big break now seemingly lost.

Arun appeared to follow the line of thought that was not spoken. "The director of the movie I am to be in is shooting around me for now. We'll see. I just don't know . . ."

Finley wanted to give him a hug, to take away the pain that so clearly threatened to overwhelm him, but she restrained herself and stayed seated.

"If you get to London, please look us up. Melinda gave us your contact information, so we will send you ours," Finley said, looking around before she continued. She lowered her voice to almost a whisper. "And if you ever want to talk, just to vent or to have someone outside your circle listen, I'm here. I can only imagine your pain."

It must have been the last comment that touched Arun because he left the bag in the middle of the path and came over to give Finley a heartfelt hug.

"I was going to marry her. We argued. She thought I was going to Hollywood without her. But I was just going early to find a place for us," Arun sobbed. "Just wanted to get past my nerves, so

I could balance work and my attention to her. Now there's nothing to balance. You have no idea how lost I feel. Melinda was my rock, my sounding board. I loved her. Now . . ."

Finley patted his hand. "If there is anything I can do to help, please let me know."

Another weak smile graced his lips. "Thank you."

Then he grabbed the bag and hurried off.

Finley sat for a moment, trying to take in Arun's sorrow, but what came to mind was the horrific way that Melinda had died. Finley thought about the *National Geographic* article she had read a few years ago while preparing for an assignment in the Amazon. It had said that, contrary to popular belief, the constriction of a boa, python, or anaconda didn't prevent the lungs from filling but rather the heart from beating. The snake's bite held the victim in place while the coils caused instantaneous cardiac arrest.

She wondered how the reptile had even gotten into the sauna in the first place. Yes, they were at the edge of a jungle, but the gardeners and staff did a good job of keeping wildlife away from the spa grounds. And to get from the edge of the grounds all the way over to the spa center before someone spotted it would have been difficult.

Someone must have carried it in. But how, without being seen? Finley pondered the possibilities. She knew she should leave it to the police, but they had made no headway. In the meantime, poor Arun had gotten no closure.

"Hello!" Finley looked up to see Naomi and her brother waving at her.

"Hi! You guys on your own today?" Finley asked as she watched them spread their towels.

Eric nodded, turning toward the pool. "My dad has a really bad migraine, and my mum is getting some sort of thing at the treatment center."

"Well, we pretty much have the pool to ourselves. A lot of people have left."

"Yeah. Mum says it's because of the murders." Naomi was matter-of-fact in her explanation.

"Well, you shouldn't worry about them. The police will take care of keeping you safe." As Finley said it, she wondered whether it was even close to true.

The kids had been playing in the pool for several minutes before she called them over.

"Sorry to bother you, but it looks like I may be getting a game room—" Halfway into the sentence, the kids erupted with cheers.

"You're going to have so much fun with it," Eric said. He looked over at his sister, who confirmed his assessment with vigorous nods.

Finley started her fishing expedition. "So, what games should I play? I'm pretty much a beginner."

Naomi rattled off a few that she liked, including *Legend of Zelda* and *Orwell's Animal Farm*, before Eric jumped in with *Pokémon* and *Super Smash Bros.*

"Danny was trying to explain loot boxes to me. Do these games have loot that you can buy and sell?"

"Some, but not like the big games like *Fortnite.*" Naomi had come out of the pool and plopped herself on the end of Finley's chaise.

"Do you play those games? Are they hard?"

Naomi scrunched up her nose and cast a glance at her brother. "We aren't supposed to play a lot of those games."

"Too violent," her brother interjected.

"But we played them on the boat. Jillian said it was okay."

"Did you win a lot of loot?"

"We sure did! And Jillian gave us some things that let us buy more," Eric exclaimed before looking around to see if his mother had surfaced unexpectedly. "We earned a lot."

"What do you do with all that loot? Does it stay in a bank in the game?" Finley was trying to sound confused by how the game worked.

"You can, but we didn't. We brought it to the store and got cash added to our account to use so we can play other games."

"Stores? Like Harrods?"

"No, they're online. It's like eBay, but just for gaming where you exchange stuff." Naomi twisted her face like she wouldn't be caught dead using anything like eBay.

"So, what are the best stores to use?" Finley asked.

"The best places are the online gaming stores like Bongo! And Omega." Her brother clung to the side of the salt pool, splashing his feet.

"Yeah, they have all the latest games, and you can use in-game money or real money to buy stuff, or you can trade in loot boxes that you don't want and they'll give you money or credit for it," Naomi added.

Finley pulled out a piece of paper and a pen from her tote. "Would you mind writing down the names of some of the ones you use."

"Sure, but they don't just sell the loot boxes. I mean you can buy almost anything there. The games, the controllers, things that make you play better. Eric likes to buy armor and shields and stuff."

"What do you buy?" Finley asked.

"Things to add to my avatars, mainly."

"Do the professional gamers use these gaming stores?"

"Sure. Esporters go into the stores for enhancements and extra lives and stuff."

"What do they do with their loot or stuff they get in a game?"

Naomi looked up from listing the gaming store names and shrugged. "Don't know. I mean Jillian is the first professional we ever met."

"Thanks. You've really been a help. Maybe once I learn a few things, we can play sometime."

"Sure. We can help you!" Naomi bounced up from the lounge chair and handed Finley a slip with eight or so names on it.

"Really helpful. Both of you." Finley wondered how Evans or Cam might be able to use what she had gathered. *They have their ways*, she figured.

"See you!" Naomi called out as she dove into the far end of the pool.

🐦 🐦 🐦

Evans and Cam knocked on the door several minutes before eight. Charlie opened the door and let them in. Finley, in a flowing abstract print dress of various shades of blue with a halter neckline, and Whitt, in an ankle-length slip dress in solid chartreuse, were sitting on the sofa, talking.

"Don't you ladies look lovely!" Cam cast an appraising eye over all three women, but his gaze rested on Charlie, who wore an olive satin draped dress that accented the red highlights in her hair.

Whitt smiled. "You gentlemen cleaned up nicely as well. What's the plan?"

Evans bowed graciously. "Nothing out of the ordinary on the plan. It shouldn't take too long. I sign and pay. We toast, then we leave. I don't want to hang around there too long. I'll use you ladies as an excuse. Too much sun. Leaving tomorrow. Whatever."

"That's it?" Finley asked.

"That's it." Evans looked over to her. "You wanted more?"

"No. I think we have had our share of dicey situations. This can go as smoothly as you like." Finley thought back on the several times when Evans or a member of his team had pulled their bacon out of the fire. "Is there any backup?"

"Not this time. Nothing besides what we bring with us." Evans grew serious. "If you don't feel comfortable, I can go alone."

"Not on your life are we letting you go by yourself!" Whitt was adamant. "Besides, we got all dressed up for this. It's not every day that we know somebody who's buying a gazillion-dollar yacht. Wish Odessa could see us now!"

Finley chortled at the image of her cousin Odessa trying to figure out how to catch a ride on Evan's yacht.

"I don't think anything will go awry, but you never know. If it does, forget your dresses, jump overboard, and swim for your lives!" Evans chuckled as he adjusted the cuff of his crisp white cotton shirt, straightened his coffee-colored linen jacket, and extended his arms, first to Whitt and then to Finley. With a courtly bow, Cam followed suit, offering Charlie his hand as they set off for an evening with Mark Sanderford.

17

WHEN THE CAR PULLED UP to the gangplank, Mark was waiting. He had added a lightweight dark-blue jacket to his usual uniform of beige slacks and a white linen shirt. The combination suited his Nordic good looks. Finley noticed that he and Evans were almost the same height and were similar in strong athletic build.

I think it would be a fight to the death if those two ever went at it. Finley looked away, putting that thought out of her head as she climbed up the gangplank. Twilight had started to creep in, giving the water the sheen of navy velvet as the soft waves undulated, thumping the side of the boat with a gentle rock. The air was fresh, with only the slightest tang of salt and seaweed.

"Welcome back! And for a truly exciting reason." Sanderford shook the gentlemen's hands and kissed those of the ladies as they boarded.

"Pleasure to be back. And so soon. I am rarely impulsive, but this seemed like a deal I didn't want to miss," Evans/Thatcher said, standing beside Sanderford as champagne was passed around.

"If I heard it right, you introduced a secret weapon during the negotiations." Sanderford gave Finley a pointed glance. "You got a very sweet deal."

Evans/Thatcher laughed a deep, hearty laugh. "The lady knew what she wanted. Who was I to say no. Apparently, Danny felt the same."

"Well, I know you and Danny still have a bit of business to transact. The girls and I will keep the others company while you talk." With that, Sanderford signaled for Anya, Lorena, and Teresa to join the group.

As usual, Teresa reserved her breath for an occasional spoken response, accompanied by a cunning smile and a cutting glance, as she lounged on the sundeck seating. Lorena, on the other hand, was more than happy to help Anya socialize.

"You guys must sail the seven seas in this thing. Where are some of the places you've been?" Finley asked when the ladies had grabbed their glasses of champagne.

"Half the places I never heard of. Singapore, Fiji, Mallorca," Lorena started. "Mark'll pull out a map and show how far everything is from Lubbock."

"Is that where you're from?" Whitt asked.

Lorena nodded. "Headed to Hollywood to make it big and decided to shift course when the breaks never came."

"So, of the places you've been, what's your favorite?" Charlie asked, bringing the conversation back to safer ground.

Anya jumped in first. "London. It's so big, and they speak English!"

Everyone laughed at her last comment, even Teresa. Finley noticed that her smile had a shorter half-life than the others, but she still responded with something other than a sneer.

"I liked Greece. All those islands—and each one is different. I remember reading mythology when I was little. Just being there was something else," Lorena added.

"What about you? What's your favorite place?" Mark was staring directly at Finley, unblinking, an undecipherable smile playing on his lips.

Finley noticed Cam's mouth tighten as he watched Sanderford through a side glance.

"There are so many great places and so many I have yet to see. My sister tells me that Luang Prabang is magical. I just went to Chiang Mai and Sukhothai again last month for another visit, and each time has been breathtakingly beautiful." Finley looked out at the water in an attempt to reduce the intensity of Sanderford's gaze. She was unsuccessful.

"But what about Salvador and Cartagena? You said you loved those cities. And all of Sri Lanka. You said you could live in Galle!" Whitt jumped in to help her divert Sanderford's laser gaze. "What about you, Mark? What's your favorite place?"

Mark turned slowly to engage Whitt. "Here. Right here on this boat!"

"But that's not a real place!" Anya challenged with a giggle.

"Maybe not, but it's my favorite place." Sanderford drew in a breath and scanned the length of the boat. "I have everything I need and can go anywhere I want."

Finley smiled. "When you say it like that, it probably can't be beat. If you tire of the scenery in one place, you just pull up anchor and sail away to another that's more to your liking."

"Not a bad life." Whitt nodded in consideration.

"Cam, you haven't told us what your favorite place is," Sanderford said collegially.

"I'm almost as bad as you." Cam chuckled softly. "Manila. My adopted home. I travel so much for work. Going around to the top resorts training. Manila may not be as pretty as some other places, but getting to sleep in my own bed is a luxury to be appreciated. Yeah. That would be my favorite."

Finley watched Charlie glance over shyly as Cam was talking. He returned her glance with a wink.

The conversation slowly took different paths as other members of the staff came out to join the party. It was almost as if it had been choreographed. From what Finley could hear, Efram was talking to Charlie and Cam about allergies. Finley suspected it was related to Charlie's work with stray animals.

Another man, whom Finley had seen a few times at the Summit and again on the yacht during the day trip, came over while Whitt and Finley were talking to Sanderford and introduced himself as Nathan.

"Nathan is my all-purpose player. He is an engineer, so when clients ask about what is going on down below, he can take them on a tour. He also is great at sales. And he oversees the control room—including the game room."

"Does he do house calls?" Finley asked. "If I run into problems on Thatch's new boat, I might want to keep him on speed dial."

Nathan laughed as Sanderford continued. "But his real contribution is to evenings like this. When we don't bring along our full kitchen staff, Nathan acts as sommelier."

"So, you are responsible for this lovely champagne." Whitt raised her flute.

"I am. It's one of my favorites, and Mark's, too. Do you know champagnes?"

Finley watched as Whitt responded. She wondered how forthcoming Whitt would be about her credentials in flat and sparkling wines. She had done all the preparation for becoming a sommelier, except the final tests.

"Some. Mainly, I just like them. Anything with bubbles," Whitt demurred.

"Want to try to guess this one?" Nathan prompted. He signaled to the waiter for a fresh glass.

"I probably am going to fail," Whitt ventured before raising the flute with its dancing bubbles to the light. She considered it for a moment. "A wild guess, but I'm going to say a vintage Ruinart?"

"Amazing!" Nathan was slack-jawed. "How did you know? Did you see the bottle as he was pouring?"

Whitt shook her head. "I'd had a Dom Ruinart once before, and this reminded me of it. I'd liked that one, and I'm really enjoying this."

Soon Whitt and Nathan were deep in a conversation of caves and grapes. Sanderford stood to the side watching the two before sidling up to Finley.

"I think we are afterthoughts to this conversation." He took Finley's arm and guided her over to a small sitting area near a gas fireplace. "I don't think they'll even miss us."

As they sat down, Cam glanced over and caught Finley's eye. She smiled, and Cam returned to his conversation.

"Is he paid for by Thatcher—or your husband?" Sanderford had seen the exchange.

"Neither. He's never met my husband, and he and Thatch are just friends." Finley adopted an amused half smile.

Sanderford leaned back in his seat and leveled his gaze at Finley. He took his time to begin the conversation. Finley gave him the reins. "I must say, Ms. Blake, that I'm intrigued. Who are you? Really."

Finley wanted to swallow her tongue. *Does he know? But how? Play dumb. Breathe. Bide your time. Breathe.*

While she quieted her body, Finley held his gaze, letting a slow, sly smile creep onto her face. She tilted her head questioningly. "Who would you like me to be?"

Mark shrugged. "Perhaps the bigger question is why are you with him?"

Ah, the real question. The game was on. Finley gave Sanderford an endearing smile. "Believe it or not, I'm a happily married woman who likes his company. He can be quite charming. We've run into him in our travels, and he never ceases to amaze—or stop amusing—me." She paused. "And he never pushes."

Sanderford flashed Finley a wolfish grin. "Does your husband know about him?"

"Are you going to threaten to tell him if he doesn't?" Finley was settling into the cat-and-mouse cadence of the conversation. It was easier to play with the truth than to think up a lie. "He has met him. He isn't threatened by Thatcher. He has no reason to be. I love my husband. Period. The end."

"Hmm." Sanderford suddenly dropped the suggestive posturing and grew serious. "I pegged you wrong, and I don't often do that."

"And how was that?"

"As a beautiful, bored, spoiled woman who had a simpering cuckold of a husband waiting at home while you jet-setted around the world with Thatcher, trying to add some spice to life."

"Sorry to disappoint you. My husband and I understand each other. I wouldn't deceive him like that," Finley said. She suddenly leaned forward. "Did you think the travel writer tag was just a cover so I could rendezvous with Thatch?"

"Wouldn't say that. I've seen your bylines in several magazines. You're quite talented."

"Thank you. I like my work, my life. I'm quite comfortable."

"With Thatcher adding the perks?"

"Thatch is a lonely man who likes to buy expensive things. He enjoys having someone along for the ride, and I'm glad to ride shotgun. My husband doesn't mind."

"Will you tell him about this trip?"

"Of course. A relationship doesn't work when there are secrets."

"Maybe that's why I've never gotten married."

Finley arched her brow. "Do you have secrets, Mr. Sanderford?"

Mark paused and smiled before standing and pulling Finley to her feet.

"We all do," he whispered playfully in her ear.

Sanderford gently kissed her hand. "I should have met you sooner."

When they returned to where the others were standing, Danny and Evans/Thatcher had rejoined the group.

"All finished?" Finley asked as she reached Evans/Thatcher's side.

He reached for her hand and tucked it in his arm. "All done. And you, my dear, have your game room!"

Finley smiled sweetly. "That reminds me. Efram, the other day you mentioned that you guys own some online gaming stores. Can you scribble down the names? I figure you guys gave me a game room, the least I could do is frequent your stores for games and enhancements!"

Efram pulled out a slip of paper and listed a few names before handing it to Finley. "I wasn't expecting that, but I won't say no to more business!"

Evans/Thatcher extended his hand to Sanderford. "I know you and your team have an early morning tomorrow, so we won't keep you any longer. It has been a pleasure doing business with you. I'm sure we're going to have a great time with that boat."

While Evans/Thatcher made the rounds thanking Danny and the rest of the team for the speed with which they had executed the transaction, Anya and her boatmates were saying their good-byes to Whitt, Charlie, and Cam. Finley saw Charlie and Anya in an animated conversation. After some exchange, Anya handed Charlie something and quickly gave her a bear hug before running below deck.

The ride up the hill to the Summit was a quiet one. Evans/Thatcher was reading over parts of the contract he had signed. Whitt was cradling the bottle of Dom Ruinart that Nathan had gifted her, and Cam and Charlie were whispering about something that Finley couldn't hear.

Finley herself was deep in her thoughts. She had just cavalierly bantered with one of the most dangerous men in the world. She had revealed little beyond the truth in her conversation. She knew Sanderford was digging for leverage in the exchange. It appeared his decision to abandon blackmail had surprised even him. All the same, Finley needed to have an honest conversation with Max about the part she had played in this sting operation. She knew he would understand, but not without serious reservation.

"So, what were you and Sanderford talking about so long? Cam said you had been at it for a while." Evans lounged in one of the easy chairs this time. His gaze was measured, his mouth positioned such that it could morph from its current easy grin into an angry snarl in a second.

"And you didn't come rescue me?" Finley feigned distress.

"From what I could see, he was more caught off guard in the conversation than you were. What did you say to him?" Evans's gaze held.

"Yeah. I was talking to Nathan one minute, and you slipped off to go dancing with a tiger the next." Whitt had emerged from her room, having changed into yoga pants and an airy linen big shirt.

"More like a cobra, actually. He kept weaving his way through the conversation. For a moment there, I thought he was going to try to blackmail me." Finley kicked off her heels and rubbed her feet together.

"Blackmail? Over what? The swine!" Cam was indignant now. "I knew I should have broken that up when he led you over there."

"Thank you, Cam, for your chivalry." Finley engaged Evans's stare and broke into a large grin. "Over you."

"Me?" Evans touched his chest. "What did I do?"

"Apparently, you seduced me!" Finley laughed at the collective gasp that went through the room. "Yes, Mark thought we were 'more than friends,' and he was angling to tell my husband about 'us.'"

"That man surely has a death wish!" Evans joined Finley in her laugh. "Max would have killed him—and then killed me! I rather like living, thank you very much."

"And what did you tell him?" Whitt asked.

"That I loved my husband, and he was not threatened by my relationship with Thatcher. Thatch liked buying expensive things, and I liked going along for the ride. No one got hurt in the process."

Evans shook his head and gave Finley an approving, lopsided smile. "Well done!"

"I decided the truth was easier than a lie."

"True, so true," Evans murmured.

"So besides having a conversation with a probable psychopath, during which I learned little besides how brilliant an actor I am, what else did we learn?"

Whitt grabbed a seat beside Charlie on the sofa. "I think Charlie may have made the biggest find this evening. Go ahead and show them!"

"I'm not sure, but I think this may be valuable." Charlie reached into her pocketbook and pulled out a bracelet with two strands of multicolored stones.

"I don't have a jeweler's loupe, but there looks like some nice stones mixed in there," Whitt said.

Cam reached for the bracelet as he pulled a small magnifier from his pocket. "May I see? Where'd you get it?"

"Anya gave it to me. She said Mark okayed it, so I figured it was all right." Charlie dropped it into Cam's outstretched hand.

Cam took his time looking at each stone. Several he returned to, holding them to the light as he examined them through the magnifying glass.

"Interesting," he said slowly, his eye still fixed on the stones. "Most of the stones are paste, but a few—like these two blue sapphires and this pinkish one—are real. And of very high quality."

"When you say 'high quality,' what are we talking about?" Finley asked.

"Probably worth fifteen to twenty thousand, total. There are a few smaller stones mixed in that would run a few hundred. And then others that are just paste. Good paste, but still paste. But two and possibly three of those stones would fetch close to five or six thousand each, if not more."

"Why would they mix the trash with the good stuff?" Finley was confused. "I mean if you believe it's just costume jewelry, you risk losing a lot of money if someone doesn't treat it right."

Evans was starting to scowl, his brows growing more knitted by the second. "But let's say you didn't really expect the stones to get into the outside market. They were just a means of transport to get under the authorities' radar."

"And then what?" Whitt fixed her eyes on Evans, who was now starting to pace.

"As importantly, why?" Charlie asked.

Finley followed Evans with her eyes as he paced up and down the length of the sitting room. He looped the space two more times before suddenly stopping.

"What if, in order to get through customs, the stones are put in jewelry that the girls either wear or dump in their costume jewelry case? They are told when they can give a piece away, no big deal. This is a rounding error if it gets lost or given away by mistake," Evans conjectured.

"That makes it easier to mix in high-value items that Mark says they can't give away. The ones that probably have stones worth hundreds of thousands rather than the tens of thousands that these are worth." Finley leaned forward as she spoke.

At this Whitt jumped up, almost spilling her tea. "And guess who gets to cut the big stones?"

Everyone turned to look at her, clueless.

Finally, Whitt spoke. "Nathan, the diamond cutter!"

18

THE ROOM WAS CHURCH QUIET. Night had fallen hard by the time they wrapped up the debrief conversation, but all the lights were on, and everyone was up. Evans and Cam were each on computers. Cam as staff was allowed to have an electronic device as long as it was kept well out of the view of the guests. Evans, on the other hand, as a guest, had to smuggle his in. Finley wondered how, with the cleaning staff and service team roaming the rooms all day, he had managed not to be detected. She suspected that the sizeable tips he regularly distributed had glued the staffs' lips shut forever.

While Evans and Cam worked at the dining room table to ensure that every detail was in place to track the money, Whitt had made them all tea before tackling a sudoku puzzle she was working on. Charlie had curled herself up on the sofa with a book in hand. Every now and then she would survey the room. Each time, her eyes would find Cam as their final resting place.

Finley had decided that now was as good a time as any to scroll through her footage and see what, if anything, she had gotten that was useable for her Asian spa story. She started with a series of pictures she had taken when they had arrived in Manila. Among the shots was one of Max with Delilah asleep on his chest. She stared at the frame for the longest time. She missed him. She thought back on her conversation with Sanderford. She couldn't imagine ever betraying Max in that way. Even if he had agreed to give her that degree of freedom in their relationship, it still would have felt like deception.

She had marked several shots of the Summit for later review. The majority of those had been taken the afternoon that Cam and Charlie had gone for their run. She had started out along that same path shortly after they left looking for good shots of the sea. On her way back she had found a flowering tree with clustered persimmon blossoms that had a black throat. She had taken several close-ups.

As such, when she had scanned them earlier, she had been focusing on the clarity of the image as well as the intensity of the color. She had paid no attention at all to the background. This time, she paused at the blurry smudge of a figure all dressed in black. The person was talking to Joseph, the snake handler, on the path that led to the staff quarters.

"Cam, may I see your magnifying glass, please?" Finley placed a finger over the image that it had taken her so long to recognize. She didn't want to have to refocus her eyes again to relocate it.

Cam passed her the magnifier and came over to see what she had found. "What're you looking at? Found a yeti?"

"Almost. What does that look like to you?" Finley needed confirmation of what she thought she was seeing. "Look familiar?"

Cam focused his eyes as he peered through the magnifying glass and moved closer to the screen. It was an awkward maneuver, one that got the attention of both Whitt and Evans.

"Why don't you just enlarge the screen?" Evans asked.

"Because it pixelates," Finley and Cam answered almost in unison. Both of them chuckled.

"The image is grainy enough because it's out of focus," Finley explained.

Whitt drew back in mock horror. "My sister took a picture that was out of focus? The shame. Oh, the embarrassment!"

"Goose, the part that was supposed to be in focus was. We are looking at the background."

"What do you think you see?" Whitt was curious. She rose from her seat and leaned over her sister's viewfinder. "All I see is a blob of black."

"And in a place where everyone—even the Blake sisters—wear lighter colors and fabrics, who is the only person around here conspicuous in her somberness?"

Whitt mouthed the answer before Finley had even finished the question. Her mouth hung open with the realization. "Jillian!"

"Where?" Now Charlie had joined the circle. Cam pointed to the blurred figure talking to the tall, thin man in the green grounds-staff uniform. It did look like Jillian and Joseph were talking. But about what?

"Mind if I have a look as well?" Evans asked as Finley passed over both the camera and the magnifier Cam had placed on the table.

"So she's having a conversation with Joseph, the snake handler. What am I missing?" Whitt went back to sit down.

"Whitt, I know it's late and you're tired, but what was Melinda killed with?" Finley looked at her sister like you would an addled elderly aunt.

Whitt's mouth dropped open as she flopped back in her chair. "Oh my goodness! You think Jillian killed Melinda with Joseph's help."

The room was eerily quiet. The jolting movement of the hands of the analog clock on the wall was the dominant sound.

"But why?" Charlie muttered, breaking a silence that had lasted uncomfortably long as the crew processed the revelation. "And why like that?"

"Melinda said they knew each other from high school. Maybe it was something connected with that?" Whitt suggested.

"But that was years ago, and they hadn't seen each other in decades," Finley reminded them. "And what sort of grudge or misunderstanding from years ago could be bad enough to result in murder?"

"As nice a supposition as this all is, someone talking to a gardener does not make them a murderer. There has to be a more proximate connection between the two. We have to find her with the snake or something close to make a viable case," Cam noted.

"Let me know if there's anything else on the camera that allows you to make that case." Evans was already back in front of his computer scowling at the screen.

⤳ ⤳ ⤳

Charlie was startled when she heard the knock on the door. It was late, very late. She got up to answer it but paused when she heard Cam.

"Wait! Can you see who it is? Doesn't matter. Let us slip into one of the rooms before you answer." He and Evans grabbed their computers and slipped into the room Whitt was using. "Be careful. We're right here if you feel unsafe."

Finley got up to stand beside Charlie as she opened the door. Safe! There had been three murders in as many days. How could anyone feel safe under those circumstances?

"Yes. Who is it?" Charlie asked tentatively.

"Sorry to bother you. It's Hunter. I was finishing with a swim and saw the lights on." His voice went soft toward the end of the sentence so it was hard to hear him.

"Hunter!" Charlie opened the door and threw it back in welcome. "Won't you come in?"

"No, I won't keep you. We're leaving tomorrow, and I just wanted to say bye." His eyes drifted to Whitt, who had remained seated but was following the conversation.

"Well, it was good seeing you, Hunter, after all these years," Whitt called out.

"Yes. This was a real surprise. Do come to a rehearsal. You're welcome to play anytime," Charlie said.

Hunter stepped through the threshold and threw his arms around Charlie. "Thanks so much. I'll definitely be in touch."

He threw his hand up at Finley and Whitt and was gone.

"What was that about?" Whitt asked when she was sure he was well away from the door. "He's like a creepy neighbor that shows up at the weirdest times. I mean, we were just talking about his girlfriend."

"Do you think he heard?" Charlie asked.

Cam and Evans were just emerging from the bedroom when Charlie voiced her concern.

"I doubt it. Things were pretty quiet when he knocked." Cam smiled his reassurance at Charlie. "I think you're in the clear."

"Speaking of clear, do we need to clear out and let you ladies get some sleep?" Evans asked. "It's going to be a long night for us."

"If you're up, we're up," Whitt declared. "We're going to see this thing through to the end."

Finley nodded. "But I do wish I had some of that coffee you served when we were negotiating."

Without saying another word, Evans reached into his briefcase and pulled out a bag of coffee. "Don't hit me because it's grounds, not beans, but I figured they wouldn't have a grinder in the kitchen."

Before she knew what she was doing, Finley jumped up and hugged him. She took the bag of coffee from his hand and started toward the kitchen. "Thanks so much! You don't know how happy you've made me."

Evans simply shook his head with an amused smile and returned to his computer.

Whitt followed Finley into the kitchen. "Looks like we aren't getting any sleep tonight."

"Nope. Thank goodness for the coffee."

"That was weird Hunter coming over tonight."

"Why? He was leaving. He saw the lights on and wanted to be sure he didn't lose touch again. Why is that weird?"

"I don't know. Too much other weirdness for anything to be taken at face value, I guess." Whitt paused, looking at her sister as she pulled out the coffee cups.

Finley stopped arranging cups and spoons on the tray to lock eyes with Whitt. "I'm going to ask you something that you asked me a couple of years ago." She took in a breath. When she continued, Finley's voice was almost a whisper. "Are you and David okay?"

Whitt took her time answering. "Yeah. Why do you ask?"

"Just a few things you said since we've been here and the way you've been acting at times. You just seem a little off. Not quite you, maybe."

"No, we're fine. Just a lot of decisions."

Whitt went quiet. Finley waited.

"Decisions? About what?" Finley finally asked, her eyes never leaving her sister's face.

"About jobs and where we need to be."

"I thought you had decided to make Manila home? Especially now that you have Delilah."

"We have, but then David has to travel so much. More than we thought he would. And with a baby, his being away becomes an issue—"

Finley grabbed her sister's hand and started sputtering. "Baby? Are you? What are you saying? Why didn't you tell me? When? Does Mama know? How are you feel—"

"Stop!" Whitt cut her off. "I'm not pregnant yet. We're just talking about it. Trying to plan. I need to plan. David not so much. But you know I need to plan."

"I know. Sorry I jumped the gun. It was just a surprise to hear you mention it. A very happy surprise." Finley kissed her sister's cheek. "And I know when it happens, it will be the right time for both of you. But don't stress about it. Plan for the contingencies, but don't stress."

"But you know David. Mr. Laissez-faire."

"Yes, I know David. And what I know above all is that man loves you. And because of that, if you tell him what you want, what you need, he will walk through fire to deliver it. So you don't need to stress."

Whitt whispered, "I know. I know."

Finley reached over and pulled her sister to her. "You and David are going to be the best parents any kid could ever have. Whenever it comes."

After a long while, the sisters parted. "I guess if Delilah loves us, we can't be all that bad." Whitt smiled and stood looking between Finley and the coffee. "By the way, how are you going to make coffee without a coffee maker?"

Finley reached under the cabinet and held up a pot. "The old-fashioned way. On the stove!"

When the coffee had finished boiling and all the cups were poured out, Finley sat on the sofa and continued flipping through the frames on her camera. Whitt had moved from sudoku to Wordle while Evans and Cam waited for the money to move. Charlie had dozed off, book in hand.

"Think we got a bite," Cam mumbled under his breath as his eyes scanned the screen. "There's movement in the accounts."

Evans refreshed his screen and saw the same. "Are you tracking it? All of it?"

"Yep, my electronic bean counter is working overtime trying to keep track of all the little pieces, but it is all adding up. There is still a large wad that hasn't moved, though."

"That's fine. It's late. Most of the movement is likely to happen tomorrow, I suspect."

The room went silent again as everyone returned to their activities. Whitt had joined Charlie in a nap.

"Well, I'll be a monkey's uncle," Finley cried out several minutes later, rousing Whitt and Charlie from their sleep.

"What's the matter? What's wrong?" Whitt was wide-eyed.

"Calm your jets, Tootsie!" Finley was tapping her viewfinder and shaking her head with a canary-eating grin. "I just found what I think is the connection you are looking for!"

"You found the smoking gun?" Evans was out of his seat and over to Finley's side in less than two seconds. "Where?"

"May I use one of the computers for a couple minutes?" Finley asked.

Evans reached across the dining table and retrieved his laptop. He passed it to Finley. "Here you go."

Finley pulled several cables from her camera bag and attached them to Evans's computer. Soon the image that was on her viewfinder was reflected on the computer screen.

"There! It is Jillian without a doubt. You can see her face clearly this time."

"Okay, we see it's Jillian, but where's the connection?" Cam had moved in to get a better look at the picture.

Finley pointed to the screen. "She's carrying a duffel. And look at what is sticking out. A burlap gunny sack. We can't see the snake, but I'll bet that if you corner Joseph, he will admit to getting paid to deliver one Jillian Sharp one large blackish snake!" Finley sat back in satisfaction.

Cam was looking at Evans. "What do you think? Enough to bring in the local inspector?"

"The picture is fairly clear. It's probably enough for them to bring her in for questioning." Evans turned to look at Charlie. "Do you think the boyfriend had anything to do with it?"

"Hunter? Unlikely. It just isn't in his nature." Charlie was firm in her response.

"People change, though, Charlie, and it *has* been several years since you knew him," Cam added.

"Yes. People change, but not that much. I just don't see it. I mean the police are probably going to take him in for questioning, but I don't think they are going to find he had a hand in whatever it is that Jillian did," Charlie said.

"Whether Hunter is involved or not, whatever you do, you need to decide fast. They are leaving tomorrow—more correctly, later this morning. If the police are going to question them, they have only a few hours or they'll be gone." Finley tapped her watch face.

"Cam, keep an eye on the money while I make a call." Evans punched some numbers into his phone and put it to his ear.

"We're juggling multiple balls here—a money-laundering sting *and* a multiple murder investigation. We'd better be right," Finley said, realizing the magnitude of what was about to happen.

Whitt laughed. "Fin, it's like double Dutch. Once you got the rhythm, you're in the flow. And we are in the flow."

19

SHE HAD WANDERED AROUND TRYING to think of ways to make this go faster, to speed the process so she wasn't left hanging for too long. They had said to sit tight, that there was a new tranche of money coming in that needed to be moved quickly. They weren't particular about how it was done, just so long as it was done with no residue. Mr. Clean clean, they had said. She knew the processes well enough, had enough networks and channels, and was experienced enough to be able to move it without a trace.

She chuckled to herself. If anyone at work knew what she did as a side hustle, they would be shocked. She held a senior position. Was well known and well respected. She regularly gave speeches about the need for integrity and ethics in tech-centric industries like banking. And no one could ever say that she wasn't one of the best at her job. Even now, she had been brought in because she was one of the best. She took pride in that.

Her phone rang, the one she used to get around the Summit's archaic rule about no phones.

"Hello?"

"It's Skywalker." As usual, no one used their real names, even if the players were all known to each other. It made it more difficult for the authorities—or competitors for that matter—to find out what they were doing. Skywalker, she knew, was the CFO. Zeus was Mark.

"Any word on when this is coming in? I'm on a plane tomorrow midday. If you want it done quickly, I need to start working on it tonight, tomorrow morning at the latest. The markets open early, so I can set up the deals tonight and execute in the morning."

"We just got it, so it's not like we've been sitting on our hands. We wanted to make sure it cleared the bank before we started cleaning stuff that wasn't ours. It's in the account. Once Zeus reviews it, you can get started."

"Why does Zeus always have to keep reviewing this stuff? It just slows things down. You have to move in this business."

"Zeus knows business. And he knows *his* business. He'll review it." The voice on the other end of the phone was trying to put her in her place. She just laughed. *I could hack into his system in fifteen minutes and collapse every deal he has pending. Don't mess with me!*

Her last boyfriend had tried that, thinking he was smarter, better than she was. He found out soon enough that it wasn't worth it to mess with her. Lost a good million plus in the process. He's still looking for his money. This one is a little smarter. He aims to please, so he won't get in trouble. At least for now.

"Zeus is on the other line. He hasn't given the signal yet. He says to hold tight for now. I'll call you when you can get started."

"You know as well as I do that this is messed up! Don't blame it on me if I have to leave before this is all done. I told you!"

"Look, I understand, but I'm not crazy enough to challenge Zeus. So sit tight. Go get a manicure or something. I'll even pay for it. Just chill."

"I'm not at the Summit now."

"Where are you?"

"None of your business."

"Sorry, didn't mean to get in your business. Just asking. In any event, I'll call you."

She listened as the dial tone returned, holding the phone to her ear long after the talking had stopped.

She ended the call and sat on the sofa, chewing on a nail. She was glad the boyfriend had decided to take a midnight swim. She would be back in the room by the time he returned, and he would be none the wiser.

"Where have *you* been?" She met him at the door when he came in. She looked him over before walking over to him and sniffing. He smelled of diluted chlorine. She didn't know what she was expecting. The smell of another woman? Her perfume or, more likely around here, patchouli oil? She had seen the hookups that were rampant—the meetings behind the palms along the running paths, the rendezvous in the workout rooms. Ben was notorious for his use of the yoga studio. So why not Hunter in the pool?

"At the pool. Where else?"

"A little rendezvous, perhaps?" she scoffed. "But you wouldn't have the nerve."

"I wouldn't do that to you. Ever."

"As I said," she muttered as she dropped into one of the over-stuffed chairs. "You were swimming this whole time? You must be a tired boy!"

Hunter smiled. "Not too tired. I took a rest after my laps. And then I stopped over at Charlie's on my way back."

"At this time of night? Whatever for?" she scowled. Was it Charlie he wanted to see or the other woman, his ex? Although she didn't seem too excited to see him. But maybe it was all an act. Playing hard to get. "They were still up?"

"Yeah. I saw their light on and decided to let them know we were heading out tomorrow. I didn't want to lose touch." Hunter looked nostalgic. "I had fun jamming with the Raiders!"

"Don't bore me with your reminiscences." She shifted in her seat as she changed the subject. "I may have to play tonight. I'll find out soon."

"At this hour? And you talk about me?"

"The difference is I get paid to do this. In any event, we need to check out early tomorrow."

"You're going to be exhausted, especially if you play." Hunter took a seat on the sofa across from her. "Why don't we sleep in and grab one last massage before we go?"

"I'll be fine, and we don't have time for a massage."

"What's the rush? Come on. One last massage. A couples' one. There's no one here, so they'll fit us in." He stood and leaned over her chair. He kissed her gently. "You know you want to. Just one last little massage together."

She reached up and pulled him to her just as the phone rang. She kissed him quickly before pushing him away so she could reach it. "You always get what you want. Book the massage. I have to take this."

"Yeah?" she whispered into the phone, her hand further muffling her voice as Hunter headed into the bedroom to take a shower.

"It's come in. The purchase cleared, and he wants you to move it fast. It's a little over three."

"And my cut?"

"If you move it within the next five hours, he's willing to give you an additional two percent."

"Make it five and I'll move it in three." She could hear the pained silence on the other end of the phone.

"You know he won't go for that."

"Ask him. If he needs it moved, he'll pay. Look, I'm the one staying up all night. Ask him."

She listened to a garbled conversation. In a few moments, Skywalker was back on the phone.

"He said you can have the five percent on condition."

"And what condition would that be?"

"It has to be in three hours. And it has to be clean, squeaky clean. If you fail on either condition, you get nothing."

She laughed out loud. "He knows he's going to have to pay me. I've never failed before, and I won't fail now. Unless one of you screws me over."

"Just clear it and you'll get your money," the man said and hung up.

She had just ended her call when Hunter walked in, hair wet, his robe open to show a finely chiseled midsection. She approached him and ran her hand across his stomach to his back. She pulled him close.

"Too bad you have to work," he whispered. "We should be having fun on our last night here."

"We can have fun later. Gaming is what pays the bills so we *can* have fun!" She kissed him hard before sending him on his way. "Book us for something fun tomorrow before we leave."

She heard Hunter put in the order from the bedroom for breakfast in bed, a couples' massage, and a late checkout.

She made herself a cup of jasmine tea and pulled out her gaming computer, attaching it to the elaborate setup that Hunter had rigged to give her a continuous stream. Over the next two and a half hours of intense competitive play in markets around the world, she managed to move all of the three million that had been allocated to her. She moved it clean, leaving nary a trace of her activities.

Later that morning, the adrenaline had her still wide awake. She had woken up Hunter after she'd finished moving the money and expended some of her energy on him. But she was still wired after her shower.

She was towel-drying her hair when she decided to check the flows on her computer. She had seen the last of the loot inventory be purchased by an esporter from Albania over an hour ago, so she was looking for her cut to be deposited into her account. Skywalker was always prompt in making the payments. When she looked at her balance, she saw that a payment had indeed been made forty-five minutes ago, but it had been reversed twenty minutes later. *What the hell!*

She didn't care what time it was. Nobody messed with her money and got away with it. She dialed Skywalker, her body quivering with anger.

"What the hell is going on? I cleared it within the limit. And I cleared every cent of it clean!" she shouted before he even said hello.

He appeared to have been expecting her call. "That's not what we're seeing. Some of it is bubbling back up. I don't know what's happening, but I would suggest you take what is left in that account and you make yourself scarce. I had to negotiate hard for him not to wipe your account clean."

"Nobody two-times me and gets away with it," she hissed.

Skywalker was talking fast in a raspy whisper. "My advice is take the money and run. Lay low. Zeus will contact you if he needs you."

She tried to cut in a few times, but the man was harried and hurried. She had never heard him like this, talking over her, his tone barbed and curt. Before she could say a word, he hung up and she was left with a blank screen. She looked back at the numbers on the computer. They had left her account with barely one percent as payment for a night's worth of aggressive play that had taken care of all their needs. Now they were ignoring hers. She'd deal with them in the morning!

She had just turned over to grab a few more hours of sleep when she heard the light knock on the door at around eight o'clock. She thought it was their breakfast. She threw on a robe and closed the door to the bedroom. She was surprised when, instead of a waiter with breakfast, it was the inspector and a couple of officers on the doorstep.

"Jillian Sharp?" the inspector asked cordially. "Inspector Guzman. I have a few questions for you if I may."

She wondered what this could be about. She had answered all his questions when they had canvassed the grounds before in relation to the murders. She had deftly deflected those. There was no way they could have any idea about any of the things she did for Sanderford. That was too far above their pay grade to even be on the police radar, she knew.

It wasn't until she saw Joseph being escorted to an awaiting police car as she closed the door, having let the officers in, that she knew the nature of the inspector's visit. Her stomach sank. She prayed that Hunter wouldn't awake until after she was gone.

But she wasn't so lucky. The police had begun their interrogation at the dining room table and had suggested it be continued at the station. They had allowed her time to get fully dressed and were leading her to the car when Hunter came out of the villa, confused.

That woman from the band and her friends, those nosy sisters, were coming back from breakfast when the police put her in the car. Hunter had followed her, calling her name and asking questions, but her brain had moved on to other things.

She would defend against the murder rap. On the other hand, she might plead guilty to reduce the police probing into other aspects of her life. She knew that if they ever found out what she did for Mark, her life wouldn't be worth a tinker's fart. She would never be safe. Sanderford would see to that.

When she arrived at the station, she was escorted into an interrogation room. Officer Guzman was already there.

"Please take a seat. We have just come across some interesting footage of you the night that Melinda Danvers was killed." Guzman cocked his head as he sat and waited.

"Interesting? How so?" She decided to probe to see how much they knew. She was going to confess, but she wanted to make them work for it. Hell, she had worked all night for a few piddling thousands. She felt like making somebody pay. Given that it was never going to be Sanderford who had to pay the piper, it might as well be this self-important cop.

"It shows you with a satchel that contained some interesting cargo. Do you recall carrying anything around that evening?"

She shrugged and sat back in her seat.

"Well, let me refresh your memory. Your friend Joseph says he delivered a package that contained the object that you had asked him to obtain for you." Guzman pushed a blowup of the snake that Joseph had delivered. "Do you remember that?"

"Maybe. It was a while ago."

"I'm sure. Joseph is helping us a lot. It makes our job easier. And we generally reward that sort of cooperation."

She smiled coyly. She knew what he wanted: her to curl up and cave, crying and begging for forgiveness like a sniveling idiot. It would be a cold day in hell before she gave him that satisfaction. She leaned farther back in her chair and crossed her arms in front of her.

Guzman drew in a sharp breath. "You can have it your way. We know what you've done. We have the evidence. So, you can make it easy. Or you can make it hard."

She watched as Guzman stood slowly and gathered the papers he had brought with him. The other officer who accompanied him also rose and opened the door to the interrogation room. Guzman turned to face her as he was exiting. "Why don't you think about it? We'll be back later to see if you have changed your mind."

It was almost three hours later when Guzman returned. He was joined by a suited gentleman with a briefcase who handed her his card. She chuckled. *So Sanderford didn't leave me hanging. Either that or he sent a spy in to see what I was saying.*

She looked up as the man sat down in a chair next to her. "May I have a moment with my attorney, please?"

Guzman nodded and left.

Needless to say, he was surprised when she asked the guard to call him back in some thirty minutes later. "I would like to plead guilty to the charge I am accused of."

Guzman frowned and looked at the attorney. The man raised his brows and shook his head. She knew that neither of them had expected her admission of guilt. She liked throwing people off guard. That was what had made her successful at gaming. In fact, successful in life.

"Why?" Guzman was staring at her now, squinting as if trying to see into her soul.

The seriousness with which he asked the question amused her. "Why what?"

"Why plead guilty?"

"Why not? Joseph gave you sufficient evidence. Besides, I did it."

Her attorney raised his hand. "Please don't say anymore."

"As you wish," she replied before looking over at Guzman and asking in a mock whisper whether her attorney was needed any longer. "Sorry. Shall I send him away so we can have a proper conversation?"

Guzman shook his head. "No. It's best that he stay."

Over the next hour, she wrote down her statement, outlining how and when she let the python that killed Melinda into the sauna. How she had waited for Ben to leave. How she had barely avoided an encounter with Arun. How she had engaged Lilith in a brief conversation right after. How she had concocted a scenario under which none of the three could implicate her without implicating themselves.

The attorney sat motionless as he read her statement. "Are you sure you want to sign this?" She knew she had made any plausible defense useless.

She nodded with a knowing look as a smile claimed her lips. She was ready to go to a cell, her new home. Sanderford had better reward her well for her sacrifice when she got out. She knew the attorney would arrange for things like food, books, and special perks during her imprisonment. She would press home to him at every chance how she had taken one for the team, as it were, so that her reward would be waiting.

Guzman reached for the statement when the attorney had finished. He reviewed it thoroughly before sighing deeply. "But why?"

"You have an obsession with why, don't you." She leaned forward and laughed in his face. "Because!"

20

CAM AND EVANS HADN'T BEEN in the reception area when Jillian and Joseph were carted away. They had headed back to Evans's villa to alternate between sleeping and tracking the money that had started to move in a thousand different directions.

Finley, Whitt, and Charlie had decided that if they were going to stay up, they needed sustenance. It was on the way back from that trip to the dining room for an early breakfast of shakshuka for Charlie and Finley and buckwheat pancakes for Whitt that they had seen Jillian being taken to the station.

It was now close to eleven, and Evans and Cam were in the Blake villa catching up on what they had missed and filling them in on what they had learned.

"Before we start on what we saw, what's the latest on the money?" Whitt was sipping on a cup of coffee that Finley had just boiled.

"All gone," Evans said, his face deadpan.

Both Finley and Whitt sat up with a start, bug-eyed.

Charlie gasped and looked over at Cam. "What do you mean it's gone?"

"Gone. Broken up and scattered around the world like ashes," Cam explained matter-of-factly.

No one said anything for several moments.

Slowly, Finley inclined her head and pursed her lips, as if questioning what she had just heard. "Ladies, I think we have been punked. That money may be scattered, but I have no doubt these boys know where every last crumb is hidden."

Whitt and Charlie turned to see Cam and Evans fighting to hold back their laughter.

"I thought we had you there for a second!" Cam had almost folded himself over laughing. He straightened up when he caught sight of Charlie, who didn't seem amused.

"Don't punish him too badly, Charlie. It was my fault! I thought it might lighten the mood." Evans appeared duly contrite. "But Finley found us out. How did you guess?"

"I have gotten to know you well enough over the years that if that money was truly missing, you wouldn't be here shooting the breeze with us. So, what gives?"

"You pegged us right. The money wasn't broken up as we initially thought it would be. It moved as lump sum and then splintered." Evans turned to look at Finley. "Just as you thought."

Cam jumped in, his voice growing more animated as he recounted what happened. "This is the first time we'd seen this variant. They used the clean money to buy a large inventory of in-game merchandise up front, just like you said. Loot boxes, swords, whatever. Then the dirty money was transferred to an in-game avatar that used it to buy game merch from that inventory, which they later traded or sold for real money."

"I'm still not understanding why they didn't just transfer the money to the avatar without using the clean money at all. They could buy merchandise from anyone and clean it through the trade without tying up the clean money with all that inventory." Whitt's banking background was kicking in.

"True, but just as Finley said, Mark wants a closed loop. With all the gaming industry scrutiny, he wants to be sure that his businesses look squeaky clean. A trace on the money from that side would show a legit transaction," Evans said.

"In addition, he gets the revenue on both the front end as the inventory of merchandise is sold and the back end as the avatar gets the money from the trade of the loot in the in-game market," Cam noted.

"Pretty ingenious!" Finley had drawn a diagram to track where the money went and where it ended up. It was pretty close to her scenario.

"Because the merch business looks wholly legit, it takes the heat off. The key is recovering clean, real money from the in-game trades. That's where Jillian came in," Cam said.

"We traced some of the in-game activity to this hotel. Jillian must have been given the task. It took only a few hours before she had sold off or traded all the dirty money in the vault and most with very little discount."

"She's good. I must say that. She is *very* good," Cam said. "She knew to try to block the initial trace, but she didn't think to attack the virus. She wouldn't have known, given how we buried it in the code."

"Yes, if we had just tried to trace it, she would have gotten past us when she bought the initial inventory. Sanderford and his team are some of the best in the world. That is how they have been able to build the empire they have." Evans reached for the coffee refill that Finley offered.

"But the biggest surprise came in the source of the dirty money." Cam smirked a bit as he relayed the story. "We were tracking both sides so when the dirty money came in, we traced it."

Cam paused for dramatic effect, but Charlie wasn't having it.

"Out with it. Where did it come from?" she asked impatiently.

"Spanky Pineda!"

Cam's revelation had the desired effect. All three women's mouths dropped open and stayed there for several moments.

Finley recovered first. She looked at Cam before shifting her glance to Evans, looking for another punk. "Spanky Pineda? Miss International's husband?"

Cam and Evans both nodded. "Spanky Pineda."

"So, his conversations with Danny were just subterfuge, misdirecting us while he conducted his business with Sanderford?" Whitt crinkled her brow and twisted her mouth as she processed the new information.

"Yes. Apparently, he has been acquiring and selling arms for a while now. Initially for rebel forces in the south of the Philippines and more recently for other splinter groups throughout Southeast Asia." Evans replaced his cup on the table and sighed. "He was the last one I would have taken as an arms runner."

"But that's the beauty of it. He came across as the abused husband who drew sympathy because of the theatrics of Miss International, and he played it to the hilt, hiding his operations beneath her massive tent." Finley shook her head.

"But what happens now?" Charlie asked.

"Now that we have the trace on the money—on both sides—and we know how they move it through the system, we will do another few trackings to bolster the case," Evans said.

"We also are looking into the other ways that Sanderford cleans his money. The bracelet confirms our idea that he also used traditional channels, so we'll follow up on those as well," Cam added.

Evans smiled slyly. "Then we'll wait until Sanderford pulls into a port where we have an extradition treaty, and we'll grab him and his team and shut them down."

"What about Spanky? You're going after him too, aren't you?" Charlie asked.

Evans nodded. "We're likely to move slowly on him so that we fully understand his operations. Then we'll move in and take him into custody."

"Catching Sanderford—and Spanky—could take months, years even," Finley muttered. "Where is the justice in that? A young woman has been murdered because she was in the wrong place at the wrong time, and another man has been killed because he used a rival's secret handshake."

Evans glanced over sympathetically. "These things sometimes do take years. Justice often moves at a snail's pace, but as your Martin Luther King said, 'The arc of the moral universe is long, but it bends toward justice.' I have to believe that, or Cam and I wouldn't do the work we do. Vigilantism would be so much easier."

Finley leaned over and touched his arm. "I suppose."

"But it isn't as dire as it might seem. Or as slow," Evans continued with a twinkle in his eye. "The security cameras on the Summit grounds caught the whole incident. The police alerted the Philippines marine patrol, and they boarded Sanderford's yacht with a warrant for the arrest of Tom Sheffield, one of the bodyguards."

"Just like that. They just arrested the guy. What about being safe in international waters?" Whitt asked.

"The boat was flying a Philippines flag, and murder is obviously an offense here, so the authorities boarded and exercised the warrant," Cam said.

"And Sanderford didn't protest." Evans arched a brow. "It appears Mark is also sacrificing Sheffield on the charge of the spa attendant's murder."

"He let one of his men be taken away on two murder charges without raising a finger?" Finley was incredulous.

"So much for loyalty." Charlie poured herself more mint tea.

"So we missed the arrest of Jillian this morning! We were glued to our computers. What happened?" Evans asked.

"Based on your call, they came over at some point during the morning and questioned her," Whitt shared. "This is according to Hunter, who was pretty broken up about the whole thing. They decided to take her down to the station to continue the interrogation.

Hunter took a cab down shortly after to see what he could do to get her representation."

"I suspect they will pull the security camera footage and have an even better view of her with the satchel." Finley hoped the cameras stopped at the entry to the spa, although frames that showed Jillian releasing the snake at the sauna would pretty much cinch the case.

"I called over to the station just a while ago. The inspector was reluctant to talk about the case over the phone, but he did invite me down to sit in on the initial interrogations of both Jillian and Joseph. At first, much of the damning information was coming from the gardener." Evans tried one of the vegan cookies that Whitt had ordered to accompany their teas and coffee. The contortions of Evans's face as he tried to swallow the concoction had the others in stitches.

"She couldn't have been the most cooperative suspect. When she was getting in the police car, Charlie heard her say something to the effect of Melinda being a nobody so she didn't know what all the fuss was about." Whitt turned to Charlie to give the details.

"I don't know if she knew she shouldn't have been talking at all, but she basically admitted to killing Melinda. Her exact words were, 'Melinda talked too much. She was a risk. What I do is worth millions. She was worth nothing.'"

"Well, she eventually talked even more. I was a little confused by her actions. Once her attorney arrived, I thought she would clam up, but quite the opposite. She pretty much pleaded to the murder charge. Explained how she got the snake—as we thought, from the gardener—and what she did. I was shocked."

"Where did the lawyer come from?" Charlie asked. "It doesn't sound like he was doing his job."

"Unless Mark sent him to get her to plead to murder so that her other work for him never came to light," Finley said.

"But what's in it for her? There isn't that much loyalty in the world that would have me going to a Filipino jail while the real crook sails off into the sunset." Whitt scoffed.

"You think it has to be an equal trade. But what would you do to save your life? Given what Sanderford will do to protect his operations, a few years in a Filipino jail, with the possibility of a prisoner exchange at some point, might not be too bad a deal," Evans argued with little emotion. Finley suspected he had seen it before.

The group was silent as they took in the enormity of Evans's statement.

"True!" Charlie frowned. "But the sad part is poor Melinda got sacrificed in the deal. A question of wrong place, wrong time."

"Apparently, Jillian tossed the prepaid phone she had used to lure Melinda to the sauna, but she threw it in the falls in a place where the water was shallow. The police retrieved it," Evans continued.

"What was her beef with Melinda anyway?" Whitt wondered out loud.

"Melinda remembering Jillian's boarding-school hacking antics and sharing them with the group made Jillian fear she might discover her 'cleaning' work for Sanderford, so she cut her losses." Evans poured himself more tea but declined another cookie.

"So sad," Charlie repeated.

"The sad part is, I don't think Jillian even realizes how sick what she did was," Finley observed. "It was all part of a business transaction to her."

"So, what now, ladies?" Evans had stood and started for the kitchen with his coffee cup.

"Leave that." Finley took the cup from his hand. "We have nothing better to do than lounge around until the car comes to get us in a couple of hours."

"I am going to lounge by our pool until then," Whitt announced. "I am so looking forward to heading down that hill and getting real food."

Finley huffed. "Whittaker Blake, I would have thought that the first thing you would have missed was your husband!"

Evans and Cam laughed at the sisters' exchange.

"Well, of course I miss him. That goes without saying, doesn't it?" Whitt looked a little sheepish.

"I don't think your sister shares that view." Cam chuckled. "When do the guys get back in from their diving trip?"

"They got in this morning. They will meet us at the harbor for lunch. You care to join us?" Finley asked.

Evans reached for his briefcase and headed for the door. "That is exceedingly gracious of you to offer, but I think my face is the last thing Max wants to see after several days away from you."

"Especially when he finds out that she spent it with you play-acting the part of your comfort kitten!" Whitt teased.

Finley whipped around to face her sister. "Comfort kitten? I was no such thing. Even Mark said he misjudged my relationship with Thatcher. Y'all's mind is just in the gutter!"

"Maybe, but I *am* curious as to how you're going to explain what happened this weekend to Max."

David and Max were waiting for the sisters when they were dropped off at the harbor boardwalk some ninety minutes later. Charlie had taken the car on to the airport for an afternoon flight back to Manila. The Four Musketeers were booked for another three days in Palawan.

"Where do you want to begin?" David asked as they sat down at Tomaso's for a drink. He had his arm around Whitt's shoulders and punctuated his sentence with a big kiss on her lips. "I cannot tell you how much I missed you!"

Max, in his typical reserve, had greeted Finley with a long, slow embrace that spoke volumes about what he was feeling, Finley knew. He had kissed her on the forehead before engaging her lips and held her silently for a long while after.

"I missed you," she whispered and received a kiss on each eyelid in response.

Now they were going to get into the details of their respective weekends.

"Why don't you guys start? You know what happens at the spa—swim, massage, yoga, repeat!" Whitt joked.

Finley could tell Whitt was trying to give Finley time to figure out the best approach to explaining their weekend. Blurting out that there had been three murders in three days followed by an elaborate sting operation that ate up three million dollars in a few hours might not be the best idea.

She listened intently as David and Max described their time at sea, flashing spectacular pictures of what they saw around the coral reefs and lagoons surrounding Palawan.

"And then the thing just turned and stared at us like, 'I've showed you around. It's time for my supper!' The most amazing experience. Ever," David gushed. Max nodded his confirmation.

Finley could imagine the two men bonding over the experience as only two who loved the water as much as David and Max did could. She was glad they had shared the time. She never would have paired them as best friends, but David had asked Max to serve as his best man, and Max had been honored to accept. They were so very different. But perhaps that was what was at the heart of their connection. Either that or the knowledge that to survive in the sphere of the Blake sisters you needed an ally, and what better choice than the man who understood the other sister best.

"We've talked enough. Tell us about your weekend," Max said.

Finley took another sip of her wine and paused. "Where do we begin?"

"Well, I'll start," Whitt jumped in. "I don't think I have ever missed real food as much. I want a big, thick, juicy steak tonight for dinner, with creamy mashed potatoes swimming in butter. Who cares if I never see another pea pod!"

Finley chuckled as she listened to her sister's description of the Summit. It sounded more like an ashram than one of the poshest resorts in Asia. As Whitt spoke, Finley's eye was drawn to the far end of the pier, where an inordinately tall man was boarding a sailboat. She watched him climb aboard and clear the ropes for cast off.

"Ms. Blake? Finley Blake?" a waiter asked. He handed an envelope to Finley. "A message, ma'am."

Finley glanced at the handwriting on the face of the envelope before opening it. She read the message and stared in shock at Whitt.

"Finley? What's the matter?" Whitt's voice pitched up in concern.

"Jillian. Jillian's dead. Apparent suicide," Finley mumbled as she passed the note to her sister. What she didn't relay out loud was the rest of the message. *Sanderford!* It was signed *Thatcher*.

Max touched Finley's hand. "Was she a friend?"

"No, just someone we met at the Summit. A very troubled person." Finley gave Max a sad smile.

As the boat Finley had seen at the end of the pier neared the restaurant landing, she saw the man come onto the deck and gaze over to where the Musketeers were finishing their drinks. He threw up his hand in greeting. Finley responded with a nod.

Max turned his head to follow Finley's line of sight, as did Whitt and David.

"Isn't that Evans?" David asked as the boat slipped past and out into the lagoon.

"Thatcher Hayes, you mean," Whitt replied with a smirk. "He just bought a yacht. And Finley helped."

"And Whitt, too!" Finley shot back.

"What?" David and Max stared at each other, confused, before looking at the sisters.

Finley turned and met Max's eye. "We'll talk about it when we get home. But not before."

Max began to speak. Finley put her finger to his lips before silencing him with a kiss. "Not before."

The End

ACKNOWLEDGMENTS

Every time I finish a book, I get excited. It's not just the sense of closure that comes from writing "The End," but also the feeling of gratitude that overtakes me. Because if it takes a village to raise a child, it takes a whole continent for me to get the ideas from my head onto the page in a coherent-enough fashion that it might even begin to be shaped into a readable story. So I would like to offer my sincerest thanks to the growing list of people who have helped me draft, rethink, and refine this episode in the Blake Sisters Travel Mystery series . . .

- Beta readers—those readers who have stepped up to take a first look.
- Book Club members—who from the first have offered their undying support and suggestions.
- Bublish team—the editors, production and distribution team, and the creatives who have helped me refine my writing and build my brand.
- Writing coaches and instructors—the teaching team in several courses I have taken as I try to get better at a craft that I have come to love. Shout out to Eva Langston, Miki Hayden, and Jeff Elkins who have read and critiqued my

work. Any mistakes are the fault of the student, not the instructor.

- Guys at Correspances—the darling restaurant near home that lets me sit and write all day, breaking only for a scrumptious lunch and a glass of rosé.
- Family and friends—my dear family and friends who are my stalwart champions in an industry where rejection is the order of the day most days.
- Readers—that growing base of "Fieldlings" who keep whispering words of encouragement that propel me to the next saga in the series.

If you enjoyed this book and want to learn
more about Finley and Whitt Blake
join our mailing list at www.mcarterfielding.com or
drop me a line at carter.fielding6554@gmail.com.
I'd love to hear from you.
Talk soon!